FINDING PASSION:

CONFESSIONS OF A FIFTY-YEAR OLD RUNAWAY

Christy Cumberlander Walker

Finding Passion:
Confessions of a Fifty year Old Runaway

Fiction: literary work of imaginary events.

Fantasy: literary work of impossible events.

Travel: literary work of destinations

This is a fictional, fantasy, travel book. It is the product of a vivid imagination and an excellent memory. I searched out interesting activities and travel tips for you to experience in the various cities listed. If you visit the cities I hope that you will enjoy the events found here and find others of your own.

While I have visited each of these cities, I did not do any of the, strike that, most of, strike that, some of the activities that I describe herein. Any similarity to any person is totally, no I mean, purely, no I mean, slightly, no I mean somewhat coincidental. Besides, I don't wear stilettos. In public. Anymore.

ACKNOWLEDGEMENTS

Primarily I thank God for the opportunity to live a dream. It is a true blessing. I would also like to thank my family for enduring. Thanks especially to my magnificent 7: April, Tessie, Two, Willie, Leon, Shaun, and MyShell. Ella and Bill, I will try not to send you to the light too soon.

If I list, all of the individuals that had an idea or a word of encouragement the acknowledgements would be longer than the book. Therefore, I would like to thank all those that encouraged me. To those who did not, I did it in spite of you. I have indeed found passion, in my own way, with my own words.

My editor is a work of art and I thank her for all of her efforts, ideas, and dedication. Christina, the only way you could be better is if you were a Christy.

I was asked if I would use my own name to publish my "travel book." I can't think of a better one. As legacies go, it is what I have to give, a piece of me in all my craziness, with all my issues. I hope you enjoy me, here. Thank you for letting me share.

It really is great being a Christy.

Contents

TRACK ONE: THE INTRO

I can't believe I finally made it onto the plane. I almost ran back to jump in the car and go home. However, I am here on this plane. I pull out my diary and start to write. I don't want to miss recording a thing.

Dear Diary,

I am so excited. I'm going on the trip of a lifetime. I'll be traveling in Great Britain for almost two weeks. I have got all of my information together, all of my bed-and-breakfast stops, and my rail pass. I'm good to go. I've even checked to make sure I have my passport in my pocket. I don't want to get locked out of the country.

This tour is a present to myself. There are about thirty of us traveling together. Since I don't have any friends who particularly want to see Great Britain, I decide to go with strangers. My friends are like me, real homebodies. I doubt if any of them have been one hundred miles outside of Wichita, Kansas, more than once.

Robert dropped me off at the airport this morning. He is such a sweet and wonderful husband. We went shopping last night for items I may have forgotten. He got me a phone so I can send e-mails from all over. He says it will keep us connected. I don't really expect him to respond, but it is really a cool phone.

I also decided to get a voice recorder. I plan to record everything worth seeing at the end of each day. That way, I don't have to write my daily activities all of the time. When I get back home, I will put all of my recordings on disc.

Then I can relive my trip whenever I want. I might even write a travel book one day about my great adventures. It will be a million-seller, and I'll go on tours all over the country to promote my masterpiece, my opus. "Travels with Lynn." Yes, a best-seller that will tell people what to see in Great Britain.

To be honest, I am a little scared of leaving all of my family and safety behind. However, I'm almost fifty. If I don't go now, I don't know when I would work up the nerve to try again.

Robert and I used to take our three kids to Colorado to brave the mountains when they were small. It didn't take that long to get there. However, with kids in the car, it was horrendous. Robert and I also traveled to Oklahoma for our honeymoon twenty-seven years ago.

However, this is different. I'm going all by myself. I get to make all of my own decisions. I feel like I'm finally grown. I can do whatever I want to, whenever I want to. This trip is about me, me, and oh, did I mention me? I'm feeling mighty liberated.

The tour guide is MyShell. We met once in person at a meeting for everyone going on the tour. She has been to the U.K., as she calls it, over twenty times. As a person to know, she is not very friendly. As a tour guide, she seems to know her stuff.

MyShell is about thirty, walnut brown with gorgeous brown eyes and perfect white teeth. She answered our questions on what to expect as if she was a schoolteacher and we were the students. I guess we are her students. Most of us know nothing about where we are going.

MyShell also assigned us partners. My partner is Hank. He is a nice person who does not pay much attention to the world going on around him. MyShell paired us up at the meeting. Our job is to keep an eye on each other so we don't get lost or anything worse. We have been given strict instructions to know where our partner is at all times. We have been told not to wander off alone, but to always, always go with our partner. It's almost like being in kindergarten, but oh well.

Hank actually lives in Kansas City. He is single since getting a divorce about a year ago. His wife decided they had nothing in common. He is not exactly Mr. Personality. He is quiet without being creepy. He looks like he has a lot of deep thoughts. Hank's therapist suggested the tour as a way for him to deal with his depressed state. I sure hope it helps.

He is short, about five feet, five inches, which would be enough to depress me if I were a man. He is in his mid thirties, somewhat cute with blond hair and green eyes. Clean cut and employed, which would be much more appealing on a six-foot frame, but we can't have everything. Besides, I hear there are women who like short men. I'm just not one of them.

Anyway, we are leaving Wichita for New York and then on to England. That will be the first leg of my adventure. From there we are going on to Ireland and Scotland. I can't believe what I am about to do. Imagine, me on a plane. I've never been on one before, but before, there was never anywhere that required me to fly.

Hank has the aisle seat on my left. I am in the middle seat, hoping that no one will come to take up the other aisle seat on my right. That way I can scoot away from Hank on my left. He seems harmless enough, not chatty or overly interested about this great adventure. However, I wouldn't mind spreading out. Hank could have crabs or head lice. I heard they jump from one person to the next infecting as they go. I would rather not get crabs or head lice on my vacation.

Okay, Diary, that's enough writing for now. I'll write more later, or tell it to my voice recorder. Here I go.

I put my notebook away and prepare for takeoff. We are almost ready for the doors to close, they say. This is good. I am feeling a bit of joy because I'll be able to get some personal space since the seat next to me is still empty. I put my blanket on the seat to my right. Now I prepare for the big scoot to the side. Joy. Joy. Joy.

Premature joy because at the last minute a man gets on. I don't notice him until he starts looking around and heading my way.

I silently pray to the airplane god. Please not this seat next to me. Anywhere but this one. Just keep it moving, sir, on down the aisle. Please. I close my eyes in internal supplication and continue sending out prayers. Don't let this be his seat, I pray to the Great Keeper of the Seats.

Nevertheless, in the way of life, of course it is his seat. He places a large envelope on what should have been my seat. I retrieve my blanket. Now I get to spend the next hours in close encounter with a possible psycho killer.

Ever on the alert for perverts, I surreptitiously study him. Cream-colored jeans, white shirt, and maroon jacket.

Okay. Harmless clothing. At least he does not have on a t-shirt that says, "I only kill people on Tuesdays." He is not very tall. At the most, he is five feet eight or five feet nine. About a buck fifty, but very nicely put together.

The way he moves is fascinating to watch. Each step is complete, purposeful, determined. He has on a hat that covers most of his face. It has a wide brown leather brim that shades and hides. He puts it in the overhead storage with his overnight bag just before he turns and sits down. Right beside me.

I have no plans to talk with him since he is a stranger, but what an interesting face. He is not really my man candy flavor, which is Hershey semi-dark-chocolate brown with lots of hair on the face. He is more of a Werther's caramel color.

He keeps his hair cut close to his head, and it is more pepper than salt. That salt holds a certain appeal allowing you to see how black the black is because of the white. Conversely, he has a small goatee that is almost all salt. The mustache is a mixture of the two and sits well on his face.

I think facial hair is an aphrodisiac. Well, unless it is growing out of the nose and ears. My husband Robert has a mustache. I want him to grow sideburns and a full beard. He will not.

This man's eyebrows are a study in black. They are so thick they look as though someone drew them on with a Magic Marker.

His eyes are pecan brown, although someone dropped in flecks of green. You can see the green if you are looking straight into his eyes. I do so just to make sure he does not look openly homicidal. I find his eyes have a slight slant as though the continent of Asia interacted with his ancestry.

Gold wire-rimmed glasses accent those eyes that are currently scanning the area. They seem to take in everything at a glance. I try to get another glimpse of the total package. His ears don't stick out and fit the size of his face. They don't have hair growing out of them. I go back to the eyes. His eyes are focused directly on me. He smiles. He saw me checking him out.

Darn. I don't want to smile back because I don't want to encourage him. He might get the wrong idea. Instead, I give him my arms length, tight, professional look. The acknowledgement looks through you without having any eye contact. It is really more a grimace than a smile in return. That should let him know to keep his distance. I am not the friendly sort.

I am satisfied with how I handled him. I promptly turn my eyes to the front of the plane. I hear a chuckle, as if he knows that I am putting him firmly in his place. He obviously finds amusement in my placement of him.

"Humph," I snort. My twenty-five year old daughter Rene, who is a massage therapist, told me not to be friendly with anybody. She said people could hypnotize you if you talk to them. Then they sell you into white slavery. She should know. She probably hears everything, rubbing on people all day. I may have nothing to worry about since I am not white. Still, you have to be careful.

"Hello again," I hear from the right side of my body.

He sounds different, which should not surprise me. I notice he does not exactly look pure African American if there is such a thing. His accent proclaims him to be from somewhere in Africa. His carriage proclaims the impact of slavery has not been imprinted on his genes. He has an extreme amount of confidence. He actually expects me to speak to him. He is a stranger.

"Hello," I tell him with a brief, "I will kill you with a pen if you try anything funny," toss of my head. My glance goes back to the front of the plane. "Hello again," he had said. I never met him before in my life. He must have me confused with someone else. That is not surprising. I look like a lot of people.

We are taking off. The plane tilts up into the air and throws my body against the back of my seat. All of my attention now focuses on trying to stay alive. I have a death grip on the arms of my seat to steady myself. All of my cool points have been tossed out.

My ears start clogging and I am sure I am going to die. I close my eyes and wait to die. After we straighten out, I peek and then open my eyes. I will not cry. People fly every day. The first thing I see is my right side row partner strangers. There is crowd of them now and they are all smiling at me as they spin round and round.

"Take offs and landings are a little rough," he shares with me.

I just nod, increasing the dizziness I am experiencing. Gradually the dizziness and the terror fade. He goes back to one face as his crowd of faces recedes.

A few minutes after the cabin crew has shared their important safety instructions, he starts talking. I did nothing to encourage him.

He looks suspect, one of those unsavory types who prey on innocent women. He may be the type who will take a plane from Wichita to New York to meet a potential victim.

I should probably take his picture. Someone will find the strange picture among my belongings. It will give the police a good place to start the investigation. They can quickly focus on him and then use the picture as evidence at his trial if I come up missing. Maybe I am a little paranoid, but that doesn't mean he isn't a psycho. I ignore him.

He just keeps on talking. He is spouting simple inconsequential chatter about the flight length, time of arrival, and other unimportant things. In spite of myself, I enter into his conversation. He was waiting for me to join in and I did try not to give in to temptation.

"Is New York your final destination?" is his question.

"I am going on a tour," is my grudging response.

Because he seems genuinely interested in what I have to say and I am so excited about my newfound freedom, I continue.

"This is my first time on a plane. I am part of a tour that is going to Great Britain. Beside me is Hank my tour partner. We are supposed to look out for each other."

Then I remember he is a stranger. He could be planning to steal my identity. I tell my mouth to stop moving. It is too late to go back to studied indifference. I opt for silence instead.

Since I decide to be quiet, he shares. They are interesting stories of events in his life. I listen. He was born in Africa and has lived in the U.S. sporadically over the years. He now makes his home in Europe, Paris to be exact, for the past twenty years. His eyes and voice invite me to take part, vicariously, in his life. Doesn't he know that you are not supposed to talk to strangers?

Another tidbit I can't help but notice is the fact he is a toucher. He is one of those people who bring you into their conversation with their words and their hand on your arm, your shoulder, and your back. It is obvious that he never took Personal Space 101.

He has his hand up, down, and around my body so much I should have motion sickness. That is why I notice his hands. His hands are intriguing. Each finger looks as though it has muscles. If he ever squeezes my hand with those fingers, he will break something.

Those hands are appearing too frequently upon my arm, hand, or knee. He always quickly removes those fascinating hands. Nevertheless, they leave an impression.

Outwardly, there is nothing untoward. Inwardly, I am becoming more connected to him than our shoulders and thighs touching should dictate. I am feeling him in an intense sensual space.

Through our dinner of cardboard with wood shavings, he keeps up a steady stream of conversation. I am barely able to choke out a response. He probably thinks I'm mentally challenged.

He informs the flight attendant of his desire to receive a Bloody Mary. Maybe he is a serial killer. Or a vampire. While awaiting the delivery, and after receiving his drink, he talks. He sips on it while keeping a steady stream of words flowing in my direction.

I am glad when he stops talking long enough to take a nap. I need to know what it is that makes me feel unsettled. I am feeling him far beneath our surface conversation. He can't be flirting with me. If he is, I am not flirting back with him.

No, I have to be mistaken. Or, I'm insane. I am too old for this craziness. It is scary and pointless. I don't flirt with strangers. Or people I know. I am married. Moreover, I have been for twenty-seven years. I must be mistaken.

Strange men don't usually approach me. I am a typical woman. Carrying about one hundred eighty pounds bone dry makes me very well rounded. I attribute that to having birthed three children and loving food.

My brown face is beginning to show that I love to laugh and there is a definite wrinkle in my forehead. I have got enough gray hair mixed with brown hair, which I don't color, and enough age in my face to testify to the fact I have been around almost half a century. Five decades. Two score and ten. I am not fresh meat.

Add to that basic brown eyes and an unassuming personality mixed with a healthy dose of paranoia and you have me. My best features are probably my smile and my terrific behind. He has not seen either of those. Everything else about me is so typical I blend in most of the time. He can't be flirting and neither can I.

I am a happily married woman. Another head toss and the affirmation that, yes, I am glad he went to sleep. If I say it ten more times, I'll believe it.

He probably does this all the time. However, I will not fall under his spell. Maybe he is hypnotizing me. I have to break eye contact if he wakes up again or I will be in a harem in India. Then they will ship me to a sweatshop in China when my body is too worn out to satisfy the lust of an endless parade of men. I can't look at him anymore if he wakes up before we land.

I could talk to Hank on my left side. After all, he is my partner on this tour. I attempt to strike up a conversation, but my heart is not in it. He seems suddenly very flat after the effervescence on my right side. Therefore, I decide to just marinate on the encounter with my row mate and remind myself how content I am with my life.

I love my job. I am an executive secretary for a public relations firm. My boss is a vice president. I have been there for fifteen years. It was my first job once all of my three children were in school. Actually, it is the only job I have had my entire life. I like it, so why leave. I thought about leaving once. But the next job might go bankrupt like Enron. I had better stay put.

The flight attendant brings ice cream. Hank and I get ours. Mr. M.O.P. (Man On the Plane) is asleep so he really should not get any. He does not hear the flight attendant offer it to him, so, no ice cream for him.

Why is she smiling at me? Wait a minute, she is holding out some ice cream.

She says, "Here is one for your friend."

Damn her for giving me ice cream to give to him. It is not as if he and I know each other.

I could say, "He's not my friend! We're strangers." I want to scream out of frustration. I just take it and smile.

"Thanks, I'll make sure he gets it," I lie to her in my pleasant voice.

There should be a rule somewhere that you can't touch someone else's ice cream. When I am mistress of the universe, I will make that a rule. I eat my ice cream, it is Hagen Daz butter pecan and very good. I notice how Hank makes short work of his also.

Touchy man continues to snooze. Ha-ha, his ice cream is getting soft.

A push on my arm lets me know Hank decides to pay attention to the world around him. The universe is conspiring against me.

"You should wake him up so he can get his ice cream," Hank says with an elbow to my ribs.

Why is everyone so concerned with Mr. M.O.P. getting ice cream? He could be diabetic and the ice cream could send him into insulin shock. Then he would die and I would have to sit next to his dead body for the entire flight. They should not even serve ice cream on planes. I am going to write a letter to the airline about this.

I make a half-hearted, very quiet attempt.

"Hey" I whisper. No response. I tried. It is not my fault. He should not be such a heavy sleeper.

He is sleeping soundly, so I can look my fill. I notice the parts that make up the whole of him. I feel the sensuality of him, imagining, fantasizing, and daydreaming.

Then a voice that you can hear in the cockpit comes from my left and says, "You've got to wake him up."

I jump, scaring myself. I think for a moment Hank can see my impure thoughts hanging over my head like the text in a comic strip. Therefore, I try again. This time I put my hand on his forearm. It feels so good I leave it there. Then I remember why it is there.

"Hey," louder, this time using my firm voice.

I watch his eyes open slowly. He had to be dreaming something wonderful from the smile that appears on his face.

I hear him say, "Yessss."

He draws it out like a cat stretching to get more good strokes from its owner. I know it is illegal to put that much bass in one word. His voice is smooth as a shot of organic Benromac whiskey with just a few drops of water. It rolls around in my ears and rests a few seconds before easing its way to my brain.

I feel the vibration as though we had shared an orgasm and it was sooo good I can only point at his ice cream with my free hand.

"Yours," I manage to croak to him.

He smiles so slowly, so intimately that I know he knew what I felt, and he felt it too. Does that make me a member of the mile high club? I pry my hand off his arm and return my eyes to the front of the plane. Again, the sound of his laughter reaches my ears.

After the ice cream, we talk some more. All the time he is still touching, squeezing, and rubbing me.

He tells me he is married. I keep my matrimonial state to myself. I don't have my wedding rings on because they are safe at home. I took them off because I did not want them stolen when the foreigners I am going to visit rob me.

He shares that he is a percussionist. Hmm, I think that means he does not believe in God. I am not going to talk to him anymore or we will both be going to hell. He tells me he is in a band. They are in the States on tour. He pulls out his notes from his envelope to share his itinerary. As though I care, and I don't. However, I still listen to his entrancing voice.

"Come and hear me play," he entices.

"I can't. I'll be out of the country and you'll be finished before I get back," is my response.

I don't want to tell him it is not a good idea for me to see him play, hear him play, or anything else.

"Sure you can. Just come and listen. Afterwards, you'll meet the fellows." I like the way he says fellows, giving each letter its own opportunity to dance around and off his tongue.

This is a bad idea on so many levels. I hear myself say "Maybe." I give him my card, just so he can have the correct spelling of my name to leave at the ticket desk. In case I come and hear him play. Which I am not. But the plane keeps flying, and we keep talking, keep touching, and keep binding.

The pilot comes on the intercom to inform us we will be arriving at our destination in about two hours. This would be a good time to tell him I am married with three adult children. Then he smiles, and I forget. Well maybe not forget. I would not care to delve too deeply into why I don't share my news. Anyway, I don't tell him.

"Come with me," he tempts as though it is actually possible. I know it is not.

So, as if I am talking to one of my children when they were small, telling them why they can't have an elephant for a pet, I tell him no. I give him the logical and rational reasons.

Only they don't include my not wanting to drop everything and spend some sensual time with him.

"I will not be here. I am going on a tour of the United Kingdom. That is why I am on this plane. I am leaving today for London." There that should get through to him.

"Stay with me until the end of the tour and then go home," comes from between his lips.

What? Didn't he hear anything that I just said? Then I think. If I could, would I? No way.

If Robert ever found out, he would divorce me or worse, turn the children against me. I would end up begging on street corners, homeless and cold. I would be pushing a cart with discards picked out of the trash. My food would be what I could find in the dumpsters of restaurants. No, I can't go with him. I am sticking with my tour.

Oh, damn. Did I forget to tell him that in addition to having three children, two grandchildren, a dog and a job, I have a husband? Said husband would kill me, then kill him, and then kill me again if I even entertained such a thought. I think I was enjoying myself so much it just slipped my mind.

Yeah, that is what happened. Therefore, I mention this cherry on the top of reasons why my going with him is not a possibility.

"I'm married," I state as a conversation ender.

"We'll only be on the road for two weeks. You are already going to be gone for two weeks anyway. "Come," is what he whispers to me while touching me too casually and intimately on my thigh. He needs to have his hearing checked.

Well, I think I already did, but I certainly can't go with him.

I tell him "I have the tour of a lifetime waiting. The U. K. is calling me. After a decent pause, I say, "Maybe."

"What is really holding you back," he asks. "I'm a harmless guy," he assures me with a squeeze on my arm.

These have to be words from the psycho killer credo to lure victims. He says them with such sincerity I almost fall for the line.

He continues, "I believe you know, as I do that this is not our first meeting. We must have been together before in a past life. The connection is there, as strong as before. Now, we have the opportunity to be together in this life. Come. I will arrange for your transportation. We fly quite a bit. I will take care of everything. All I want is for you to be with me. Again. Come. Enjoy it for two weeks. Let's see where it goes. Come." He rubs on my upper arm and the back of my hand as he talks.

Hmmm, I have a husband, you have a wife, and it will not be going far I think to myself.

We are touching down. Truth to tell, I am sad that our interlude is ending. It has been as exciting and unexpected as it has been interesting. I will be walking away from this with much more energy than when I got on the plane.

What if it did last two weeks? It is not like a passionate love affair. It would have a definite end. He lives on a different continent, so we would not be running into each other on the street.

Why not? I think to myself. Ummm, maybe because I am married is the answer. I am sure I have more sense than that. I can't go running off like some kid. I am not completely or even slightly irresponsible.

"Yes, I'll go with you."

Did those words actually come out of my mouth? I am excited about it. I don't even want to take it back. The smile on his face helps me know that I made the right wrong decision.

So I immediately say, "But you have to agree that for everywhere we go, we will go to or see something a tourist would. After all, I'll be missing my tour."

"Okay. I'm willing to do whatever you like."

We shake hands to seal the deal.

"There will be a car waiting for me at the airport to take me to the rehearsal spot. Then you can go on to the hotel. I'll be there later." He takes my hand, holds it firmly, smiles and says, "Yessss."

So what happened that could cause a 49 -½- year old, solid, reliable, secure, loving wife and mother such as me to walk away from hearth, home, and a trip to Great Britain? It was all the fault of this man on this plane. I should probably take the bus from now on. However, I doubt this experience can possibly happen twice in a lifetime.

So now, instead of being a traveler, I will be a runaway. As a teenager, I thought about running away. I discarded the idea. The love of security kept me from hitting the road. I have always been the reliable one, never impulsive.

The worse thing I used to do is curse like a sailor. It is something my best friend, Kadijah, and I used to do when we were in school. It made us feel rebellious.

We used to have curse contests. Whoever lost had to buy ice cream. That way we were always winners. She lost on "liar bitch." We both agreed that it did not make any sense and there was something about a noun-verb agreement. But, it still sticks in my head.

My personal favorite was "cock sucking son of a bitch." I thought it was very expressive. We used it for a few weeks, calling it CSSOB. We had just come up with two more we thought were keepers, "ass wipe" and "bitch fucker," when my dad overheard us at play.

We got a talking to about acceptable language. Dad said people who have a limited vocabulary or have nothing important to say use profanity. He expected better from us. I wanted to tell him to stick a dick in it, but he would have beaten my ass. Anyway, that effectively ended the profanity game.

Then when I was grown and could curse with impunity, I met my future husband, Robert. He told me cursing was unladylike. He would not want to kiss anyone with a dirty mouth. I stopped actively cursing. I did have my priorities.

However, I have a store of curses repressed if I ever need them. Now, looking back, I am returning to my younger years. I am running away. I don't really know where I am going. It will be two week of adventure.

What about Ms. Guide Lady MyShell? What can I say to get out of this tour? The truth is not an option. I don't think she will believe that I just changed my mind. What am I to tell my straight-laced tour partner Hank?

I could say "Hey Hank, remember that guy who was sitting next to me on the plane, who I know absolutely nothing about, other than what he told me? You know the one I woke up so he could get his ice cream and I could almost have an orgasm from hearing him say "yessss?"

Well, I'm going to be going away with him for two weeks instead of being your partner on this tour to Great Britain that I saved up for a year to pay for. Would you like some extra rail passes?"

In the end, I decide on the illness standby. After we land, I seek out MyShell.

"I am really not feeling well," I start the conversation.

"I'm sure it's just the flight," is her response.

"No, I think it is something more. I am feeling so unlike myself," I tell her. That at least is the truth. "I think I should go home." That is a lie. "I need to see someone." There is truth again. "I think it would be better for me to not continue on to Europe." I don't know if that was the truth or a lie. I am sure I will find out in two weeks.

"Well, you know the ticket is not refundable," she asserts.

"Yes, I know. I'll see about getting a flight back." In for a penny, in for a pound is my thought.

"Well, is there anything that I can do to help?" she unconvincingly puts forth.

"No, but thank you so much," I absolve her.

"Would you like me to call your husband?" she throws over her shoulder as she is walking away.

"Oh, no. He would just worry until I make it home. He's got some relatives here in New York, I'll call them," I explain. Sweat appears on my forehead. I start to feel truly ill. "There is nothing you can do. I will just get my luggage and make those calls. You just go ahead with the rest of the group. I will be fine. I promise."

"Well, if you're sure," is her response on a note of relief.

Finding Passion: Confessions of a Fifty Year Old Runaway

"I'm positive" I assure her. I am turning into such a liar.

I walk with the tour group to get my luggage out of baggage claim. I am explaining my situation to Hank and accepting his condolences. I feel ever so guilty and excited inside. That is until my insides think about the adventure that is ahead of me. Then they cramp. I think I really will be sick.

He is waiting at the other side of the luggage carousel, hat firmly in place, watching me. How well do I know this man? Not very, only about five hours worth. But damn, I feel so connected to him we must have been lovers in a past life. Now I am entrusting myself to him in a fashion. It feels as though I have done it before. I grab my one suitcase off the carousel, aware of his eyes still on me. They make me awkward and secure at the same time.

As I watch the members of the tour group gather their luggage and head to the international gate, my thoughts are so clear. Great Britain will always be there. The opportunity for another time to see it will always be there.

This man, this time, will never happen again. I am going along for the ride with him. For as long as I can remember, life has been happening to me. Now it is time for me to happen to life. I roll my suitcase and carryon to the other side of the carousel. Towards him and an uncertain but exciting future.

TRACK TWO: NEW YORK

As we make our way through the seething mass of humanity that is present at John F. Kennedy airport, we are holding hands. It is as though we need to touch each other. It is unusual being this close to a stranger. It feels nice, just holding his hand. We make it to the doors.

There is a short white man who must be the driver holding up a sign with Mr. M.O.P.'s name on it just outside of the baggage claim area. We go to him and Mr. M. O. P. introduces himself and me to the driver. The driver takes over our luggage and leads us out to a black Lincoln Town car. Once inside the car, he starts talking to me about the tour. The excitement in his voice is infectious.

About an hour from the airport, the car gets to the rehearsal drop-off. Mr. M.O.P. takes a wad of bills and puts them in my hand.

"You may want to go shopping and buy some things," he tells me and then kisses me softly on the lips.

He tells the driver to take me to the hotel. Then he gets out and disappears into the large brick building where the driver has parked. I don't know what to make of this.

A quick count shows it is about four hundred dollars. Am I a prostitute? I did not have any physical sexual contact with him so I guess not. Maybe it is a deposit for services to be rendered. He may have overpaid.

The driver continues on to somewhere. He stops at a hotel after driving about twenty minutes further and gets me out with our luggage. The bellhop comes and loads everything onto a cart. I head inside to the registration desk.

I give my name to the registration clerk. My seatmate had already called so that I could get a key. The clerk welcomes me and tells me how to get to our room.

The room itself is nothing to write home to describe. This is a good thing since I can't write home about it. It is just a bed, closet and bathroom. There is not much in the way of furniture. There is no high-speed Internet connection so I can't even check my e-mail except through my phone. That is probably a good thing. I am supposed to be in the air traveling overnight tonight.

After about an hour, I am going stir crazy second-guessing myself. Maybe a walk around the area will calm me down. We seem to be in the middle of somewhere with activity and I recall seeing shops. I decide to head down to the front desk to get some information.

***

Condom Questions

Back out on the street, it is still light out, only being around four in the evening. I make my way to the right for two blocks and then hang a left. The desk clerk has assured me there is shopping in that general area.

I know I can't use my credit card. That is how the police tracked the killer on the CSI show. If I use my credit card, they will find me. I need to get some sunglasses so people can't see my eyes, that way they can't identify me when the police circulate my picture.

I'll just use the cash he gave me and not feel guilty. Whoring is not easy and it is not assisted by naturally occurring paranoia, either.

As I walk, my mind is working furiously asking me questions. Am I supposed to sleep with him tonight? I really want to, but that seems so sluttish. What are the rules nowadays?

When I was dating Robert, it was quite a while before we did anything other than kiss or cop an occasional feel. My best friend Kadijah, the curser from my youth, has a time schedule. Before she will allow a kiss, they have to have two dates. After two months, touching starts. Everything else comes after six months.

He and I don't have six months. We only have two weeks. I am ready to give him a titty touch just for the smile he gave me. Unfortunately, I recall my titties are not much to touch. It would have spoiled the moment. Whom do you ask about this? I can't call any of my single friends because I don't want them to know I ran away.

By the way, should I buy condoms? Who has the responsibility for that? I am so out of date. Then, who puts it on?

Shit, when I was younger, this was not an issue. Why didn't I meet him 30 years ago? I remember telling the children to use condoms and the whole safe sex talk. I sure as hell did not know what I was talking about in my sex talk. I am glad they didn't ask any questions.

I see and enter a huge pharmacy. I decide I'll get some condoms in various sizes, just in case. I quietly ask a worker where to find these items.

"Condoms are in aisle twelve at the end on the left side," he shouts.

Everyone in the store is now looking toward the front to see who needs condoms in the middle of the afternoon. I look even more conspicuous walking quickly toward the back. Bastard, he does not know the meaning of the word discretion.

I make it to aisle twelve without incident. What the hell is this? They have more types of condoms than grocery stores have candy. They have ribbed condoms, lubricated (with and without spermicidal) condoms, and lambskin condoms. What do you do with that? I don't want lambskin in my nether regions.

Look at that, they have flavored condoms. If you eat the condom, doesn't it defeat the purpose? Glow in the dark and colored condoms. Do white men use these to imitate black men and vice versa? Does it really matter what color it is? You won't be able to see it once it gets inside. Maybe each color feels different.

Ultra sensitive or non-latex. Hmmm, maybe I should get those in case he is allergic to latex. If his parts swell up, he would probably be pissed. My friend Dottie is allergic to latex; her hands get welts and swell just from touching it.

What if I am allergic to latex? My vagina would swell up and we would have to go to the emergency room. They will have to call in specialists to separate us. The hospital will call my insurance company. The insurance company will need to tell the hospital if they cover vaginal separation or penis removal from a vagina.

That will make the news. Everybody will see me. They will know that I am not in Great Britain. I will be in a hospital in New York with a swollen vagina that some stranger on a plane can't get his penis out of because of a latex allergy. Okay, no latex.

I could get 'his pleasure' or 'her pleasure' or the kind that heat. I don't think I want heat in my nether regions either. I mean what if my "area" starts burning. I know that's what happens if you have a venereal disease, so heat does not sound like something I would want. And, that's not even all of the condoms.

Maybe I should not get condoms. What if he wants to get a little bit? Damn, I would like to get a little bit a lot of times, but now that I am here, it does not seem like such a good idea. I wonder if I can catch up with the tour.

We should have had the sex talk. How would I start the conversation? "Excuse me Mr. Man On the Plane that I just met. Since I am coming on this journey, do you expect to have your way with me? Can I have my way with you? Just to clarify, who is the one responsible for getting condoms?"

Maybe he is one of those people that don't use condoms. My daughters would know the protocol, but I don't have a clue. I think I saw a show where the condoms are in the nightstand drawer beside the woman's bed. I don't know why they went to her house to have sex, but I am out of touch.

Okay, I am getting some damn condoms and putting them under the pillow. At the appropriate time, I will just pull it out. I am sure he will know the drill. What size would I get anyway? Small, medium, large. Oh. The sizes are regular, magnum, and well hung.

Maybe I should get all sizes, just in case. I should have copped a feel so I am not too disappointed. I probably could have felt him up on the plane. I remember seeing on the Discovery Channel or reading that feeling a penis while it is at rest can be deceiving. If a penis feels very big regularly, it does not have any room to grow when the penis gets excited. A strategically placed blanket on the plane and voila! I would not be having this conversation with myself now.

Who am I kidding? If he had put a blanket over his lap, I would not have touched him. I am not a toucher, but I love to be touched. I am starting to get angry that he put me in this position. He should have been much more specific about what to buy with the money.

"Buy some things." That is not any type of real communication. We're already having communication problems and we haven't been together a full day. I could have stayed home for this shit. I leave the store angry at my own stupidity and his inability to be clear in his instructions. I also leave condomless.

Back at the hotel, I am bored out of my mind. I am much too hyped. I can't eat anything with my stomach jumping up into my throat. The telephone rings and my naturally occurring paranoia kicks into high gear. It must be Robert. He has tracked me down to this hotel room with some man I don't even know. I had better not answer it.

Common sense tells me that Robert would call my cell phone if he wants me. Therefore, I may as well answer the phone. I can always say it is the wrong number. I like it when common sense kicks naturally occurring paranoia's ass.

"Hello," I answer in my very professional voice.

"Lynn, how are you?" I hear the voice of Mr. M.O.P. ask me in an 'I wish I was there' voice.

"Fine," I answer with a smile. He can't see my smile, but I know he has to hear it in my voice. My condom pique is forgotten.

"We are taking a break from rehearsing. I wanted to call to see how you are doing," he purrs.

How considerate. I could learn to like this. "I'm just getting back from a walk." I decide to leave out my condom distress.

"I called to see if you would like to come out to the rehearsal tonight? I can send the car back for you. We'll be here late tonight going through everything," he tells me.

"As much as I would love to, I think I'll pass, I need to rest up from the flight," I inform him. "I don't know how I would have survived a flight to London. This has already wiped me out."

"Okay. Have a good rest. I'll try not to wake you when I come in."

He does not sound angry or upset. There's no guilt trip, no argument, just understanding from him. I could really learn to like this.

I hang up the phone and grab a shower to relieve my tension and to get rid of travel funk. I complete my voice recording promise next. I thought I would be too nervous to sleep, but around midnight, I put on my so unsexy nightgown and climb into bed. I am asleep almost immediately.

I don't even hear him come into the room or get into bed with me. He was considerate enough to let me sleep thorough his entry.

***

Meet the Fellows

The next morning, I am up by eight the clock beside the bed tells me. He is still asleep in the bed next to me. He does not appear to have on any clothing. His chest is bare and clearly visible so I look.

Nice firm chest, slightly hairy. That should feel good against mine. I could lift the sheet to look further down to see if he is naked on the bottom. I am too much of a chicken.

I wonder if we had sex. I should have been able to feel something if we did or this is going to be the start of two disappointing weeks. I should have had panties on. Then I would have felt him taking them off.

Since I was sixteen, I never sleep in panties. I had heard somewhere that you should let air get to your pubic area at night so you don't get an infection. Your area gets to breathe and let the air cleanse it. That made sense to me then. It still does now. It does nothing for my current plight.

I look for other hints or signs that there had been sexual activity. I can't find any. Maybe he is waiting for this morning to pounce. I watch him. It is pleasant because he is calm and inviting even in his sleep. His breathing is even, untroubled. Looking at him as he sleeps reminds me why I made this decision to leave with him. Pure selfish pleasure.

After some length of time spent watching him, it seems as though he feels me watching. As on the plane, his eyes open slowly but he is completely alert. He is looking straight at me and I can't look away. Again as on the plane, he says one word.

"Yessss," making it a question.

How can one word hold such emotion? Right there while I am watching, he smiles. It seems beautiful to me. I can't say anything. There is no ice cream to point to with my free hand. I just get out of bed to run to the safety of the bathroom. I hear his laughter behind me.

I feel more in control once I have my street clothes on. I am even more relieved when he has completed his morning ambulation. I notice that he sleeps in boxers. I still don't see a damn thing, not that I was looking. Now would be a good time for the sex talk, but I don't know how to start it off.

Thankfully, the door lets loose with a loud noise not long after he has dressed. From that time on, one by one, the fellows come up with a reason to see him. Thankfully, only three others are involved in this rite of passage.

The first is Willie who plays the keyboard. He needs to check on the time that the van is supposed to leave for the gig. He stands about six feet two inches and I would put his weight at around two hundred forty pounds.

He says he is from the Midwest, but there is a slightly shady air about him. He does not talk much and probably knows more secrets than any one person should. He is pleasant and nice looking in a rugged sort of way.

I would say he is around fifty to fifty-three years old. He is just starting to gray in his thick black head of hair. He wears it corn rowed without looking in the least effeminate. It hangs down his back.

Ten minutes later, Leon needs to borrow some deodorant. He plays bass, guitar. He looks about forty-five to forty-eight years old. Brown skin with sleepy brown eyes and from Kenya, he stands about five feet ten inches. Boy, what a charmer.

He kisses my hand and professes himself pleased to meet me. He has charisma, and is pure hound dog. He looks like he would put the moves on any open hole available. I think Leon would charm a toad if he could get it to stay still long enough to stick his dick in for a quickie.

Shaun the sax player is the last to show up. His excuse is he can't find his overnight bag. Forty-two to forty-five years old, he is the youngest looking. He has jet back hair that has beautiful waves.

A little on the thin side and from South Africa, he is neat. He seems to be the most open of them all. He has a wicked wit about him that makes me laugh as he describes the rehearsal last night.

We all spend time in the room for about an hour. They must have received some signal from him because they all make their adieus after telling me how much they enjoyed meeting me.

"So do I pass inspection?" I ask with a smile.

We laugh and then he puts his arms around me for some kisses. Wonderful kisses. Thoughts of my condom episode intrude. I decide to take the bull by the horns. If I could feel his horn, we would not have a problem. We are going to have the sex talk. Easier said than done. I chicken out. I am not the most aggressive female I know.

Mr. M.O.P. and I decide to go out to a nearby Chinese restaurant for a late breakfast. It is just a few doors up. It is helpful for me to get more space between us. The short walk helps me to focus on what I want to say over breakfast.

Thankfully, it is not crowded, only six or seven other people eating. This should not take long. I am spending an inordinate amount of time looking at the menu. I don't want to admit that I feel as nervous as I do. I really want to talk about our sexual arrangement or lack thereof. I just don't know how to broach the subject.

He asks me "Do you eat meat?"

Great he brought up the subject of sex, now we can have the sex talk. Seconds before I respond, I realize he is talking about our meal.

"Well, yes, as a matter of fact I do. Do you?"

"Sweetheart, I eat everything," is the answer, accompanied by a mischievous smile.

Maybe we are having the sex talk. Time to look at the menu again.

The waiter comes to get our order. I get egg drop soup and shrimp egg rolls. Rice before noon would probably clog my throat. Shrimp toast would not have been any better. My mind is on him eating everything. He has the General Tso chicken.

He wants to share, which I think is adorable. With a lot of conversation and more handholding, we get through another meal together. Unlike our meal on the plane, this one does not taste like cardboard.

Afterwards, we walk back to the hotel. He puts his arm around my waist. His hand must be hard to hold up because it starts to slide towards the south. It is a good thing my ass is there to stop it from completely falling.

"Do you know your hand is on my ass?" I question, calling his attention in case he did not know.

"Yessss."

We keep walking. I don't even see what we are walking past. My attention is on my ass with his hand on it burning a hole through the clothing.

Once in our room, he gives me our itinerary so I can plan the tourist outings. It seems long and involves a lot of airport time. I look at where we are going:

New York: Tuesday –Thursday

Lobby call Wednesday 4:00 p.m.

Airport for Cleveland 7:00 a.m. Thursday

Cleveland: Thursday 10:05 a.m. – Friday

Lobby call Thursday 6:00 p.m.

Airport for Nashville 5:30 a.m. Friday

Nashville: Friday 7:35 a.m.–Monday

Lobby call Friday 7:00 p.m.

Airport for Las Vegas 8:00 a.m. Monday

Las Vegas: Monday 10:54 a.m. – Thursday

Lobby call Tuesday 7:30 p.m.

Lobby call Wednesday 7:30 p.m.

Airport for San Diego 9:00 a.m. Thursday

San Diego: Thursday 12:10 p.m. - Saturday

Lobby call Friday 6:00 p.m.

Airport for Phoenix 8:00 a.m. Saturday

Phoenix: Saturday 10:43 - Monday

Lobby call Saturday 4:30 p.m.

Airport to New York 9:00 p.m. Monday

Finding Passion: Confessions of a Fifty Year Old Runaway

New York: Tuesday 6:44 a.m. Tuesday end of tour

The timetables help the fellows to plan any extracurricular activities, such as myself. If a person is late being in the lobby, they have to pay a hefty amount as a fine, no excuses. This assures that they will be where they should be, when they should be there.

A band tour has all the makings of a great vacation. I have not been to any of these places. I will be broadening my horizons. It really is better than hanging out with Hank. Besides, there is no chance this kind of attraction could exist between Hank and me.

I can feel coldness emanating from him. He is drawing away. It is as if he is going into himself, preparing to do something. Maybe this was not such a good idea. I should get his voice on my voice recorder so the police will know where to start their investigation. He may be plotting to torture then kill me. Even though he is physically here, he has gone so far away. Like Elvis, he has left the building. Therefore, I stop trying to talk or interact with him. He is checking his watch.

"Is there something wrong," I ask him. I am a bit confused and I have to find out what is going on with him.

"No, I'm just getting ready for tonight. We are doing two sets tonight. We do one at six and one at nine. I am running through the songs in my mind. I need the quiet to hear the music so I can play it," he tells me.

That makes me feel better. "Oh, I'll just give you some space, I tell him."

At least I know it is nothing I have done. When Robert gets angry, I get that distancing. Then I have to guess what I have done wrong so I can apologize. I give him the quiet he needs.

"Thank you. I'm glad you understand," he says and then gives me a hug and a kiss. He goes back into himself and whatever is running through his head.

***

Smoke, Coke, or???

The clock shows we should be in the lobby in thirty-five minutes. The only person I have not met is the tour manager. Marty is a Jewish guy that I catch up with in the lobby at the appointed time.

Marty acknowledges our introduction with a disapproving nod of his head. He probably thinks I am a groupie I think to myself. Then I realize he is right. I am a groupie.

Marty herds us into the van and drives us to the venue. On the way, Mr. M.O.P. tells me that there are usually drugs involved. He and the fellows don't get into that scene having learned lessons early on about the aftermath of drug use.

They prefer the natural high that music provides. He does not want me to be surprised. We get to the club so everything can be set where and how it should be. We'll have a quickie meal before the set with the owner and then we will eat a meal after the last set.

It is rather strange being in an empty club. The place is quiet as a cemetery. Daylight refuses to shine into the place. The artificial lights just make the space even creepier. There are tables that seat four, set with white tablecloths. Six tables seat eight up front with reserved signs on them.

Once setup and sound checks are complete, we go into the owner's area. It has a professionally decorated touch. It is very tasteful, with fruit cornucopias and wall hangings all over.

I hope he never has roaches. They would look like seeds from the watermelon in the wallpaper. Off the entrance to the left there is a kitchen area with a full bar. To the right is the sitting area that has a beautiful red leather couch. The matching chairs and tables give an opportunity for group conversation. Off to the sides are tall tables where you could perch on equally high stools to get away from the people in the center of the room and have private conversation.

All of the activity seems to be around the sitting area. Substances are plentiful. They offer me a variety to partake. The owner has things that are a veritable smorgasbord of illegal activity. They should keep this hidden out of sight just because so much of this stuff in one place will certainly give you a contact high. There is a plethora of drugs, most of which I know nothing about.

I am not stupid. In my teens and twenties there may have been some illegal drugs in my vicinity. People smoking marijuana or doing things that would cause police to take interest was in my distant past. I actually know people that do pills, for their nerves of course. I know what coke looks like, but DAMN. Some of this I had only seen on television or in the 'this is your brain on drugs, don't take it' ads.

I have not smoked weed since high school. I had to give it up because it interfered with my naturally occurring paranoia. I know how to roll, but when I rolled, or watched other people roll a joint, it looked like weed.

This shit looks like you are taking your life in your hands if it touches you. I don't know if you are supposed to sniff, smoke, shoot or take some of this stuff orally. Actually, I don't know how to shoot and that is probably a good thing. Therefore, I very politely decline. I have a ways to go to get used to the music scene.

In order to appear social, I accept a bottle of spring water that I can open myself. I would not want anyone to put LSD on the top. When I drink it, I would become high and jump out of a window. I need to be alert. They may decide to make a virgin sacrifice. Virgins being so very hard to find, they will make do with me. I have to remain alert. I always tell my children "you really can't be too careful nowadays." I am following my own advice. No drugs for me.

I take a seat at one of the tall tables. I am away from the action so I can see if Mr. M.O.P. is a junkie who will surely murder me in my sleep once the beast is unleashed in him. The incense burning gives off a nice scent. It must be chamomile because it is soothing. I am just sipping water and getting mellow. I must still be tired from the plane ride. Everyone else is in the middle of the room. I am the sideline observer keeping myself pure and free of mind-altering drugs.

Finding Passion: Confessions of a Fifty Year Old Runaway

I am looking at my legs through my brand new blue pantyhose. Pantyhose are a necessary evil for a professional woman in the Midwest. They are as needed as a standard blue suit, with navy pumps. When I was getting dressed tonight, I put on pantyhose since I was wearing a dress.

I also know that pantyhose are inherently evil. I have been in important meetings, ready to stand, walk, or greet, only to feel the feeling of nylon becoming train tracks down the front, (why not the back? Because pantyhose are EVIL), of my leg. This is what occurs in the right leg of my pantyhose as soon as I cross my legs on this incredibly high; I think it is growing, stool.

In solidarity with my right pantyhose leg, my left pantyhose leg gets a small hole that starts a long and involved trek from Central Africa to Florida. I can feel the strands as they begin to unravel. I watch. It feels rather liberating, creating space for my leg to expand. I watch this journey unfold right before my eyes. Bits of flesh appear between the nylon. How interesting.

Okay, I hope the club will be dark and no one will notice. What else could happen? Well, how about an itch on my right leg? I have no other earthly alternative but to scratch that itch. I try to ignore it, but pantyhose are evil. They intensify the itching sensation.

And so, discreetly, I scratch. I end up making a hole the size of California. Pantyhose are ungrateful Sons of Bitches. Of course, it is directly on the knee. The hole joins the fun of the train tracks and works around to the back of my leg.

Like most women (maybe), I have the pantyhose that I only use for pants. They have the hole that will surely show in a skirt. I can hide them safely under slacks. However, I have on a dress. The hole is showing. In fact, the only thing that is holding the top of the pantyhose leg to the bottom of the pantyhose leg is about fourteen strands of nylon.

Well, I'll keep them for when I wear slacks. I consider this as I sit by my untainted self away from the drug abuse going on in the middle of the room. I barely notice that he is still holding a glass with amber liquid. His glass does not seem to get a refill. I guess he is not an alcoholic. Nevertheless, I am watching. Just in case.

There is a point that the body reaches where you are so high, you are just back around sober again. Like people who are so intelligent, they are totally stupid. Or so stupid they think they are intelligent. It may be that you are so high you think you are sober. I am quickly, effortlessly, and unknowingly heading to that point.

Sitting there, I discover your pantyhose will talk to you. This should have been the tipoff that I might be way too high. I don't know how I got high. Maybe they put something in the water. I opened it myself so I must be sober. What if they used a hypodermic needle like the lady did on that one show where she killed her husband. That is my naturally occurring paranoia coming to the forefront.

Common sense checked out a little while ago. Ergo, maybe I am so high I am just right back around sober again. I did not take anything to get high. I don't feel high. I must be sober.

"Psssst!"

Since I am sitting away from the action, I look around to see who is trying to get my attention. Of course, it is my pantyhose. My pantyhose, in conjunction with my naturally occurring paranoia have me at a decided disadvantage.

I look down and ask, "What do you want?"

The left leg, the bolder of the two speaks up. "I think they are planning to kill you."

"That's bullshit," I yell.

The right leg pipes up, "It's true, and they look homicidal. They are over there plotting. They are musicians after all."

I glance over there at them. Sure enough, they all look slightly homicidal. They are also all staring at me. Everyone has stopped talking. In fact, all conversation in the room has ceased except for my bigmouth pantyhose.

"Act natural," I say to my pantyhose.

"What do you mean act natural? They are going to kill you. Then blame it on us. They will wrap us around your neck. We'll be the cause of death," the right leg whimpers.

"We don't want to give pantyhose a bad name," Lefty screeches.

"Would you please shut up?" I tell them both.

Silence from my legs reigns and gives me the chance to assess the situation. I lift my head and look into the eyes of a group of strange looking men. I act natural and stare at the ensemble in the middle of the room. The best defense is a good offense. If I climb down from this ladder, I might be able to make it to the floor and from there out of the door. What am I doing on a ladder anyway?

"Well maybe they won't kill you," says Lefty.

I breathe a sigh of relief.

"They will rape you."

That comment doesn't exactly make me feel any better but what can you expect from pantyhose.

"Yea," chimes in the right leg, "they will have sex in every orifice. Then they will rip us off in a fit of unbridled lust. We will be useless to stop them as they have their way with you. This is going to get ugly."

The seat of my pantyhose pipes up. "I don't want any rough stuff. You know you can always depend on me. The legs are always starting shit. I won't tear. The crotch and me are always here for you. It's those damn legs you've gotta watch out for."

"So what am I supposed to do?" I ask legs, crotch and seat.

"You'll have to go on the offense," orders my bolder left leg. "Okay, throw the lamp over to the corner, and run to the door. Then whip out your cell phone. Call the police as you run screaming from the room. Do you remember seeing it on that one show you were watching that one time?"

Hell, I don't even remember my name. I'm seriously contemplating eating the grapes on the wall because I'm hungry as a hostage. Why in the world would anyone put grapes on the wall? They could have put them in a dish the way most people do. I think the owner just hung these grapes and other food on the wall to be different.

How do you get a watermelon to hang on the wall? This must be a magical room. A room where the food just hangs on the wall. I decide to see if I can find some chips. I think about climbing down from the ladder.

"Pay attention," demands my left leg.

"We'll get you out of here," whispers Ms. Right.

"Throw the chair at them," commands Lefty. "You can take them." My left leg is very supportive.

I gingerly turn around to climb down from the ladder. Once on terra firma I announce to the room "I think my left leg is on crack." Then I go back to my perch, seconds before I remember I meant to get some of that food off the wall.

That is about the time my brain and ears decide they are mad at each other. I know this because while my ears allow me to hear everything around me, I can't hear anything I say.

"Hello" I call to test my theory. I don't hear a damn thing. Maybe I am going deaf like Helen Keller. Maybe my lips are not moving. I put my hand on my mouth to see as I say "Hello" with more effort. Still don't hear a thing. I will have to talk with my hands.

I may as well start practicing now. I focus on making words with my hands. I don't know sign language and have to guess at it. The only sign I know for sure is the middle finger so I say it or sign it to the ensemble.

"Oooh, watch out, he's coming at you from the right," screams my left pantyhose leg.

Suddenly Mr. M.O.P. is beside me. "Don't you think you should move away from that smoke?"

"What, the chamomile, the incense," I think I ask him.

"That's not incense. It's hydro, purple haze."

Isn't that a Jimi Hendrix song? Naturally occurring paranoia does not mix well with hydro purple haze.

"What the hell is hydro purple haze? I need to know what is going to kill me. What did I ever do to Jimi Hendrix? I don't like guitars anymore," I share with him.

"Marijuana, reefer, smoke," he solicitously explains.

"What! You mean I have been sitting here inhaling marijuana reefer smoke? It must be crack. I am beginning to feel addicted already. What if I'm allergic? I could have an asthma attack."

He asks in a voice full of concern, "Do you have asthma?"

"Well no," I admit.

"Allergies?"

"I don't think so. I didn't when I left Wichita," I think I tell him.

My pantyhose rally me. "He didn't know that," they shout. Both legs in tandem.

So I tell him, "I could have had asthma, you didn't know that. Then I would be dead. You all would have taken my body and stuffed it into a garbage dumpster so the cops would not find me.

My family would never have known what happened. Dogs, rats, and cannibals would eat the flesh from my bones. They would not even put my face on a milk carton because I am old. I'm already age enhanced." Naturally occurring paranoia does not mix well with marijuana, reefer smoke.

It is at this point I decide I really need to eat. The grapes in the cornucopia on the wall look appetizing. I turn to climb down from the ladder again to head over and get some. Unfortunately, they still are not real and they still are a part of the wall. As I try to grasp them in my mouth, he kindly but firmly escorts me to the couch.

The boys in the band kindly move and shift to get as far away from me as possible. It is as if I am some sort of psycho chick and they are the normal ones. Hell, they are the musicians! Who could be crazier than they could? I give them the evil eye, which would have been much more effective, if I could focus. My eyes sided with the panty hose and crossed, ruining the effect.

"Lie down here and I'll be back for you when we finish the gig," he suggests.

"Now it's coming," Lefty screams. "I told you we should run."

"Kiss my ass," I think I yell. My ears are still messing with me. I will never wear pantyhose again. They talk too much.

"I am a crack whore," I maybe scream. That is my last rational thought, if you can call that a rational thought, before Morpheus comes to take me in his arms.

I don't recall anything when I wake up in bed at the hotel room the next morning. Then pieces of memory dance around. I am alone. I would not blame him if he left me here.

I am getting nervous because I'm in a strange city in a strange hotel, alone. I take a quick glance around the room. His bag is still here. Maybe he doesn't think I am a complete nutcase. Then I hear the door open and close. I decide cowardice becomes me. I act asleep. I try to get in a snore or two. It does not fool him for a second.

"I know you're not sleeping. Would you care to talk?" The voice is comforting.

"No, I don't think so. I am going to pretend that I went on my tour. Right now, I am in London. You can't see me. I didn't make a complete fool of myself last night. It was all a bad dream. When I open my eyes, you will be MyShell, the tour lady."

When I open my eyes, he is sitting on the bed, still looking as appetizing as he sounds. I close my eyes again. The universe did not hear my declaration the first time. Perhaps it will now.

"Are you there? MyShell?"

"It's still me and we still need to talk."

I bite the bullet and give in to the inevitable. "Okay, I'm awake. What do you want to talk about, the weather maybe? Pretty crazy weather we are having around here isn't it?"

"Well you were pretty wasted last night. Is this normal for you? We really try to stay away from the drug scene. It's bad for the music."

I explain. "No, I am not a full-fledged junkie. I am not even a half -fledged junkie. I am not a junkie at all. I try to stay away from mind-altering drugs."

Thus begins our discussion about drugs. After we finish talking about drugs it is going so good, I decide we might as well have the sex talk. "Since we're talking about sex," I begin.

He interrupts me. "Were we talking about sex?"

"No and that's the problem. I think we should talk about sex. Are we going to.... you know?"

"You were always impatient. Would you like to?" he asks as he bends in close to me on the bed, shrinking the available space.

"I don't know. Sometimes I would like nothing more than to strip you naked and have uninhibited sex with you. But I don't really know. I have been monogamous for over twenty-five years. Now I'm wondering when and what to expect."

"I'm a patient man. Anticipation is an aphrodisiac. Besides, it's not time yet." As he is talking, his hands roam over my body. Testing, touching, exciting.

"Well, I don't want to be caught off guard."

"Put your guard down. Nothing will happen that you don't agree to have happen. Trust" Then he kisses me and leaves me wanting more.

I get out of bed as he stands. Because it feels right, I walk into his arms. He holds me close and I feel content.

"We are due in the lobby in forty-five minutes," he tells me in our hug. What a downer.

I go to grab a shower. I know the airplane will be cold and dress accordingly. I take time to talk into my voice recorder. If I ever think I have done anything stupid again, I will just turn on this message about last night to remind me it could have been worse. Once ready, I decide to go to the lobby. I have to face everyone so I might as well get it done.

When we are all gathered, I start with "Hey guys, about last night, I'm sorry. I'm not used to…"

They quickly interrupt. "No need to explain," comes from Willie.

"We've all had times…" from Leon.

"You were fucked up," says Shaun.

"I just want you to know that was not the normal me," I explain.

"Well whoever it was sure was having a good time. How many of you are there in that body?" This comes from Leon.

"Well I didn't know that was marijuana," I defend myself.

"I used that once on the police in Texas. They didn't believe me," remarks Willie.

"I mean it. I just want to say I am sorry. It will not happen again." I loudly insist.

"I used that once on a wife I had," says Leon, "she didn't believe me."

"Would you please shut up?" I yell.

"I remember one of those people in that body said the same thing last night. But it wasn't you, right?" asks Willie.

Shaun comes over and hugs me. "No mind baby, forget about it."

Leon says, "No mind, it's okay."

Willie laughs, "It's cool."

Marty doesn't say a word, just walks out to the van shaking his head with a disgusted look on his face.

Mr. M.O.P. comes over and caresses my hand. "You didn't have to apologize; they won't hold it against you."

"But will you hold it against me?" I ask him.

"The only thing I will hold against you is me." He tells me as he gathers me in for a hug.

That sounds like a winner to me. We walk out together for the ride to the airport. He squeezes my hand before putting his hand on my waist for the eventual slide south.

I feel better for attempting to face the situation head on. I feel good because I think he knows how horrible last night was for me, and truly does not hold it against me. I could learn to like this understanding and acceptance.

Maybe he is hypnotizing me while I am with him. I did not know you could think if you were hypnotized. Maybe it is just a longing on my part.

We catch our nine a.m. flight to Cleveland without incident.

***

My travel Tips for New York

If you find yourself in a nightclub on 167th Street that is a venue for great music, don't go to the owner's area. And bring your own condoms.

TRACK THREE: CLEVELAND

We arrive in Cleveland at five after eleven in the morning. The plane ride was not bad. I must be getting used to take offs and landings or this was an easier plane ride. Ever efficient Marty has the van waiting. We are staying at the Holiday Inn on Snow Road not far from the airport. The drive is uneventful. Personally, I am still half-asleep although I am trying to pay close attention to where we are in case I ever get the opportunity to come back.

Once at the hotel, we go to the lobby. Marty gets us all checked in and gets everyone's room numbers. Marty comes back and passes out room keys. We each get a key to the room and head that way. The room is pretty basic, a desk, bed, and mirrored closets.

The television is in a cabinet that has three drawers at the bottom. That way you leave your underwear and other things in the drawers when you check out. Everyone forgets to make the final check to ensure they have all of their belongings. The hotels then make a fortune selling left behind items.

After we are settled, I look around for something to do. I go back to the desk area. The clerk says there is shopping at the mall across the street and suggests we go down to the Flats, an area by the Cuyahoga River that is a tourist attraction.

When we get there, we can catch a cruise on the Nautica Queen, a ship that sails the river and Lake Erie. They provide brunch and entertainment. I get a brochure for more information. Today they will have a rehearsal in the evening. Tomorrow they will play a set.

The cruise looks interesting so I make a telephone call and garner information on the two o'clock start and four-thirty end times. Mr. M.O.P. says he needs to pick up some things at the mall and will be happy to have some time on the water when I share the plans for today and tomorrow. He calls Marty's room and asks for permission to use the van. Marty gives a positive response, and the admonition not to be late for the meeting in the lobby at seven.

We decide to go across the street to the mall. We don't see anything particularly interesting. I am still not used to being around him so I walk around, look around, and try not to be nervous. We eat in the food court and talk about our respective views on shopping. Mostly we just look and smile at each other.

We head back to the hotel and he prepares for rehearsal. Once he leaves, I go out and walk around again. I am wondering what the hell I am doing here. I know better. This has got to be the most irresponsible thing I have ever done in my entire life. Well, at least I have not had sex with him.

It is getting dark so I go back to the room. There is a message on the telephone from him asking if I want to get something to eat. He leaves his number and I call him.

"Sweetheart, are you hungry?" he asks when he answers the phone.

"No. I am still full from lunch at the mall. I am really tired so I think I will just go to bed," I tell him.

"Okay. Well, call me if you need anything or change your mind. I miss you."

"I miss you too. I may be asleep when you get in. I am still kind of tired," I tell him.

"Does that mean don't wake you up," he asks on a laugh.

"Umm, umm, well," I stammer.

"Sweetheart, I am joking. You have nothing to fear from me. I'll be back when we finish," he tells me.

"I'm not scared," I lie. "If I'm up when you come, we can talk."

"Honey, I want you to be up when I come. And I want you to come too. Goodbye for now."

I can't think of a response so I look at the telephone to wait for inspiration. It starts making the hang up the phone noise, so I hang it up. He is okay with my decision. I get to stay here.

I turn on the television to make sure that there is not a missing person's report filed that sets off a massive search for me. I am not on the news so I decide to go to bed.

***

On the Water

The next morning, we are in bed together when I wake up. It is mid-morning and he is sleeping soundly. Once again, he was considerate and left me to slumber.

I go to take a shower and get ready for our day. I decide to wear my flowered pants that would declare me a tourist even if I were in my own back yard. They have green palm trees on a red background that somehow made sense to me when I packed them. A nice red peek-a-boo top with Keds tennis shoes completes my ensemble. I think I look cute.

I don't want to disturb him so I decide to go for a walk so he can continue his rest. We have some time before we need to go to the cruise. I walk around the hotel and see the sights. I think about our day adventure and go back to the hotel. They have a business center I use to get directions.

When I go back into the room, he is up and dressed. Mr. M.O.P. opts for a green polo shirt, brown denim slacks and brown leather sandals. I think he looks cute too. We are ready to head out for our adventure.

I use MapQuest directions from the Internet and help from the desk clerk to get us to the Flats. It is not far from the hotel and I don't mind driving since he does not have a valid driver license for Ohio or any other state.

Ten dollars gets us parked in a place a few steps away from our destination. The clerk told me that if I park anywhere else, I might face a ticket, and impound of the van. Marty's words make the cost of parking at a parking lot seem worthwhile.

A short hike gets us to the cruise ticket office and the boarding area. It is funny how he holds my hand as we walk across the parking lot and onward to the Nautica Queen our ship for the day. I remember doing that as a teenager, but not since then.

I have to stop to give myself a sharp much-needed reminder. No comparisons. This is a two-week vacation. Vacations are always better than life at home. Don't get it twisted.

The ship can hold over one hundred fifty people on three levels. It is blue, white, and beautiful. Before we board, the crew takes our picture in front of a ship steering wheel. Probably so if the boat goes down, the authorities can identify the casualties. This is reassuring.

My picture may end up in a book on the sinking of the Nautica Queen. It will be one of the great naval disasters of the Cuyahoga River. We will rank right up there with the Titanic sinking. We will all go down with the ship. Steven Spielberg will make a movie about us and Loretta Devine can play me, the leading woman.

Not being a sailor, I say to the crew, "I want to stick close to the entry level."

They lead us to a table where we take our places on the water level. Our table is a four seater. We decide to sit beside each other so we can have private conversation once the ship leaves the port. We also have a great view of the water. It is very calm as it slaps gently against the side of the boat. The spray is warm.

Our tablemates make it on board the ship. We learn they are celebrating their fourth anniversary. They look to be in their mid forties. They are very ready to spend time with each other, which is great. Mr. M.O.P. and I can spend time with each other without appearing rude.

The servers come and let us know when it is our time to graze at the buffet. We both load up. Eggs, bacon, French toast, more pastries than you should sample, carved roast, bacon and ham. It is a veritable feast. Once back at the table, we set about enjoying the view, the food, and each other.

Of all things, we talk about religion. He is a Catholic, which seems out of place. After all, he is a musician already and an adulterer, almost. At least he is not a pedophile.

I share that I am in between religions, which seems appropriate. All of my life, I have been very active in churches. Lately, I have not been making the effort. Therefore, that must be why satan has come to tempt me and my flesh is definitely weak, but our connection is so good.

Satan is probably busy tempting someone who matters or, hanging out with George W to pump his ego into starting another war in a third world oil rich country. I may as well enjoy this time because it is passing. As someone once told me, "Life is short and then you die."

The view from our portal is fantastic. The shore and part of the city are on display like a picture. The weather is cooperating. It is warm without a cloud in the sky. The food is filling. The conversation is stimulating. We are primarily interested in each other.

The intercom has someone droning on about the sights along the coast. As the ship glides out from the Cuyahoga River to Lake Erie, we finish eating. Then we trade stories about our children, our dreams.

Later we order a bottle of wine. While we sip our smooth Riesling, we walk up the staircases to the observation deck on the third level. As I look out over the water, he stands behind me with both arms around me, holding me close. I lay my head back against his shoulder. I allow myself to be soothed by him and the water. We stay that way until the heat from the sun eventually drives us back inside.

We go down one flight to the second floor and in to the music area. There, a disc jockey is spinning country, R&B and everything in between, trying to earn his paycheck. We go in to hear the sounds. I have a slight aversion to watching people without rhythm dance, but with Mr. M.O.P., everything seems special.

True to form, the disc jockey plays a chicken dance song that has rhythm-less people crowding the dance floor in seconds. Music is a beautiful thing. The disc jockey gets his wits back or gets disgusted seeing what I saw. He puts on a slow song.

Luther is singing "So Amazing." It seems right for us to get onto the dance floor to hold each other in what could pass for a dance or a simulated sex act. Between Mr. M.O.P. and Luther, I am ready to be vertical. We dance some more and then make our way back to our table on the first floor. All too soon, the cruise is over.

Heading off the ship, the crew tells us to stop so we can look at our pictures. The photo taken as we got on board is there for us to purchase. We were smiling at the camera like cheesy tourists. Mr. M.O.P. hands over a twenty. That gets us a key chain, two five by sevens, and four of the wallet size pictures. He gives me a five by seven and two wallets. He really likes the key chain. We probably should not have pictures, but what the hell.

Walking back to the van, his hand is making a slow slide from waist to ass. We get to the van before the walk becomes indecent but have to wait while the van cools down enough for us to get in. I did not know it would be this hot in Cleveland. I had a wonderful time.

I ask him, "Was it too bad for you?"

"Being with you will never be bad for me," he tells me as that sexy smile appears. The smile spreads, as my legs are ready to do if asked.

How do you respond to a comment like that? Nothing comes to mind so it is better to keep my mouth shut, get in, and start the van. I'm glad I'm driving; he might have us on the wrong side of the freeway. We ride out I-90 and I-71 South to get us back in time to refresh ourselves before the gathering in the lobby.

I grab a shower because it is definitely sweaty out there. I am in need of refreshment. As I get out, I remember that we have had the sex talk. It is getting late. It's better to have got it out of the way. I come out of the bathroom, wrapped in a towel like a mummy. We may have had the sex talk, but I am naked and he is a stranger. He smiles before going into the bathroom. I can have some privacy while he gets ready for the lobby call. I get dressed in record time.

As he gets out of the shower, my alert paranoia goes off on high alert. He may try to grab me. Then I get distracted. He feels no compulsion to cover-up like a mummy. He is in front of the mirror watching his own self, so I watch too. I notice he takes very good care of his body.

He looks as good with his clothes off as he does with them on. His body has markings on his back, chest, wrists, and upper chest. The marks are about one quarter to one half inch in length and wide as the head of an ink pen. They are in groups of four and mirror each other on either side of his body.

"What are those marks? They are too uniform to be accidental," I say to him.

"This is what tells my people who I am. These are my tribal marks. If something should happen and no one could identify me, these marks will tell where I come from and who my people are. It's a part of my culture, my heritage."

That makes more sense than a driver's license to me. I continue to watch. I am jealous of his hair. He conditions it as he is standing there in the mirror. He closes his eyes as he firmly rubs the conditioner into each strand. He moves his hands across or over his head as if he loves the sensation. It looks so good to me; he must be getting off on it. I am. I am just sitting on the bed watching. I never thought I had voyeuristic tendencies. Obviously, I do.

He opens his eyes to see me watching or rather drooling as he applies lotion to himself. "What?" he asks me.

"Nothing," I mumble then turn away.

After a few minutes he asks me, "What is your passion?"

"What? My passion? I don't have a passion." What a weird question to ask I think to myself.

"You don't think you have a passion. Sure you do." He has a way of making certain questions into a statement. "There is something that burns in you. Everyone has a passion, the thing they do that they can lose themselves in, that allows them not only freedom, but also unity within the universe. What can engross you, bringing you joy, solace, peace?"

He continues, "Musicians are accepted as having a passion because it can be heard. Other artists are known to have a passion because it can be seen. But everyone has a passion." He seems surprised and sad that I don't know what I am lacking.

"I don't have a passion," I reiterate.

"If there were no worries about money, time, and family, what would you do to occupy your time?" he asks.

As I try to stall to think of something worthy, I already know the answer. I just don't want to share with him. I don't want him going into my soul, discovering the parts of me that I don't want shared.

In a small sheepish voice, afraid of scorn, comes the admission, "I would write."

"What would you write?" he asks with all of his attention, as if the answer is important.

"I don't know, probably some of the stuff that comes into my head. The words run around so fast, that I can barely remember them. That used to happen a lot when I was younger, but it doesn't so much now."

I lay back on the bed to get away from his attention. He has stopped doing his hair to focus his attention on me. I am not used to this much intensity and scrutiny.

"When the words come into your head, do you capture them on paper?" He waits for me to answer.

"No I'd have scraps of paper everywhere if I did that," I scoff.

"But what if you just write them down? Keep them, find your passion, and release your passion. What would happen then?" He is moving closer to me.

"I don't know." It scares me to think about it. I don't want to put that much of myself out. I start moving away from him, needing the distance.

"Write something for me." He reaches out to turn my face to him. I am starting to like looking directly at him to see the response to my words in his face. It is freeing until he starts seeing too much.

"I can't. I'm not a writer." This discussion needs to stop.

"Sure you can. What would happen if you give yourself the freedom to find passion? Let it come. Before we part, share your passion. Write something for me."

"We'll see," is my non-committal answer.

That effectively ends the conversation. It allows me to escape. But it was not really an escape. I can see in his eyes that he has an expectation that I don't want to live up or down to depending on my point of view. Or to have myself be the object of ridicule if I open myself too much. For me writing is too personal to share. I try to ignore the message in his eyes and turn to prepare for tonight.

It's exciting because tonight will be the first time I see him play. I recognize some of the music even though it's not my favorite genre. I am riding to the gig with them so I have to be ready early.

I dress in my cute dress, sans pantyhose. It is a blue number that has a swinging neckline. The fabric is soft. It sways with my every move. Low blue heels that match the shades in the dress set it off perfectly. I am ready at lobby call time without a minute to spare. I get appreciative looks from all but Marty.

***

In His Passion

The club is on Clifton Avenue. A jazz club where they also serve dinner. The fellows are all famished so we will have supper before the set. I get a deliciously rich lobster with pasta dish. Mr. M.O.P. has steak. His meal is not adventuresome dining but it comes with great presentation and flair. The steak with bright yellow corn and green beans looks appetizing. Of course, we are sharing again. I don't even pay attention to what everyone else is having. I just know he and I are here. Eating. After supper, they all leave to do the set-up for tonight

They come back when everything is set. We sit around laughing, talking, and trading stories. Just before show time, the group leaves to go to the owners' area. I decide to hang around the show area until the gig starts. I don't really care for owner areas anymore.

I wave them off and think I hear a collective sigh of relief from the fellows that I will not be in a position to inhale again. Even though I would be vigilant, discretion is sometimes the better part of valor.

The club is filling up. The crowd is mostly white and across the age spectrum. I am glad I am already seated halfway in the back, able to see everything, with a nice glass of cabernet.

The owner strides onto the stage. He gives a rousing introduction to the full house. Then the band comes into the area from the same doors the crowd had recently entered Mr. M.O.P. stops to give me a quick kiss as he and the fellows pass.

They take their places to begin with some music from their new album. The crowd loves the sounds the group is making, grooving, clapping, and enjoying. The solos give every member of the band the opportunity to be heard individually. Each of the band members is extremely talented to my ears. The sum of the parts is mind-blowing. I watch him and can see his inner peace. He is so in his element, I don't think he sees the people out here, including me. The look on his face shows he is totally in the music.

I did not realize exactly what a percussionist did but see he has some small drums along with some other things that he carries in his bag. I took that to mean he was a drummer. But there is a wide selection of percussion instruments. I learn that tonight as I am watching him and see why his hands are so intriguing.

He has a drum covered with string that he puts under his arm to play; a small double drum that he beats like it stole something. He has various other instruments that make beautiful sounds when he touches them. He touches them so often, so intimately that the visual is as good as the auditory. He is just there, living in the music.

As the band descends into their older music that I recognize, he drifts even further away. I don't know what he is hearing, but the sounds he is making are beauty. The fellows transition seamlessly from one song to the next.

The few songs that have lyrics are in a language I have never heard before. The songs could be about setting the building on fire, then shooting everyone who runs out. It sounds so damn good I want to join in. However, I don't understand what they are saying much less how to pronounce it.

On fast songs everyone is on their feet, swaying, swinging, smiling. On slow songs, the sounds almost make you cry because of the intensity of it. The music transcends language, time, and age. I forget my wine on the table as I fall into a deep musical trance. It is by turns exciting and tragic. The energy in the room is tangible, connecting everyone to each other. It is absorbing in the nature of a George Clinton concert without the drugs. This is life being so damn good.

Now he is beating congas that come almost to his chest. He is playing the hell out of them. I know what they are because I remember Desi Arnez playing them in "I Love Lucy." I think the movement of his fingers explains the muscles in his fingers.

He is slapping the congas, making a multitude of different sounds. It sounds like there are two or three people back there with him helping him out. A resonation lasts after his hands have moved on to another instrument. By turns loud and soft, the varied metal objects he hits with sticks are effectively calling attention or adding other punctuation. A question mark here, a comma there, or an underline for emphasis.

He looks up straight at me. In a way, he looks straight through me and everyone else. He is in his own world. Then he gives a head toss to let me know he is back. He is aware that I am here watching him. He smiles larger than I ever saw him smile. Then his eyes close as he leaves again. He is definitely in his passion. I envy him that, putting himself out there and not giving a damn what anyone else thinks. He is getting his.

After the two hours of wonder are over, I keep sitting, still watching the stage even after they have left the room. Gradually my attention shifts to the people who are in the room with me, listening to their conversations. All are hyped.

"Wasn't that great?"

"I saw them before."

"It was moving."

"They always do an awesome set."

I need a few minutes to get back to being alone in my skin, separating myself from being at one with the crowd. I toss back what remains of my cabernet. I continue to sit. Finally, I stand to make my way to the front of the building, shedding my fellow audience members with each step.

The fellows are interacting with the crowd, receiving their just accolades. There is a large amount of hand pumping, bear hugging and cd selling going on. After about twenty minutes, Marty starts herding them to the van. I am feeling extremely insignificant, an imposter, with no right to be a part of this group. I have no particular talent other than eating chocolate with almonds.

The ride back to the hotel is full of noise, but I can't find words. I am unnaturally quiet. Mr. M.O.P. asks, "Are you okay?"

"I'm fine, just really stunned by how great your music is live," I tell him. "I understand now what you mean by passion. You really have a gift."

He smiles. "Everyone has a gift." He holds my hand the entire way back to the hotel and down the hall to our room.

"What did you think about the gig?"

I think I wish I had something that I love to do half as much," I confess.

"But you do. You just have not given yourself the freedom to do so. Allow it to come. It will. The key is to accept it when it does come. Respect your gift whenever, however, wherever. Use it, welcome it, and find your passion."

He showers before climbing into bed with just his boxers on. "Are you coming?"

"Later," I tell him. He is asleep before me tonight. I sit in the chair to watch him breath. As I sit there, I think about my experience. I think about passion. I test opening my mind to the words. Sure enough they come. Thoughts of being a spectator at the gig, being a part of the audience, being a part of the him, flow through me. I find my passion then start to write:

IN YOUR PASSION

I saw you in your passion tonight
I watched you
Giving

Receiving
It was incredible to see
To hear
To experience
The music moved you in ways no human ever could

I saw you in your passion.
You were so there
 Away
Unreachable
I glimpsed your soul
It was so intense I wanted to cry.

We were as one
But I doubt you will remember my name.
Or my face in weeks to come
I am one of legions that have succumbed to your allure

But
I saw you in your passion tonight
And I thank you
For I will never forget

I feel purged and put my writing to him in his drum
bag. I can go to bed now that the passion is out. I do a
combination of voice recording and diary writing to capture
the time that defies confinement before crawling in bed
next to him; I wish I could be one of his instruments so he
would touch me like that.

He wakes me up to get ready at five forty-five for our
lobby call. Our flight leaves at seven for Nashville,
Tennessee. I am glad we are staying so close to the airport
because it means a few more minutes of sleep.

He gives me a gentle nudge before he whispers in my ear. "You really have to get up so we can make it to the airport."

I reluctantly climb out of bed to prepare myself for the plane ride to our next location. We make it to the lobby with two minutes to spare. Then we head onward to the airport to be a part of the early morning business travelers. It is a quiet ride. I think all of us would have welcomed a few more hours of sleep. We make it through security without incident. We find our seats without difficulty.

Once we are airborne, Mr. M.O.P. takes my hand. A squeeze has me turning to look at him.

"Thank you," he says.

"For what?" I stall. I don't want to talk to him about my writing. It is too personal.

"For sharing your passion with me," he says. "Have you ever thought about writing for others, sharing your passion?"

"No, I couldn't do that," I tell him.

"What is holding you back? I felt moved by your words," he says.

I don't want to talk about it because I am feeling too vulnerable. "It was nothing," I say.

We both know my remark is a lie. I am getting very concerned that this may end with me somehow getting hurt.

I feel him too deeply, but that is something to worry more about later. I pretend to go to sleep. I don't want him to see any further into my soul. I keep my eyes shut and don't have the horrible experience of takeoff and landing that I did previously. Maybe it is the knowledge that he is beside me.

***

My Travel Tips for Cleveland

Take the brunch cruise on the river. It's cheesy but fun. Check out a club that has good music and become one with the music.

TRACK FOUR: NASHVILLE

We arrive in Nashville at seven forty-five on Saturday morning. The airport is large and busy. Marty has us wait at the baggage claim area while he secures the van. Everyone is bundled in with the help of a skycap and we are on our way to the hotel. Marty says it will only be a short ride.

We are staying at a nice spot off I-65 near the airport. As we enter the lobby, there is a rack loaded up with brochures of things to do in Nashville. I grab a colorful brochure for Jack Daniels distillery in Lynchburg. Since we have a free day tomorrow, we should enjoy it.

I figure we may as well go see how whiskey is made. That will fulfill my tourist curiosity. There is a number listed on the brochure to call for the free shuttle service. None of the other people has an interest in the distillery. I talk with Mr. M.O.P. and we decide to go just to get away. We get our things together then head to the room.

As he opens the hotel room door, I jump because I see someone moving in the room. However, it is just our reflection in the mirrored closet on the wall directly across from the door.

Our room has a mini-kitchen and living area. The bathroom is to the right of the door. The ugly green satin sofa is beside the closet to the left. Next to the sofa is a small matching upholstered chair. Still further left is a huge bed and another mirrored closet. There is another door to the left of the entry door. It must lead to another room.

The two rooms together can become a large suite. I check to make sure the door is locked on our side so no one will come into the room while we sleep. I don't want to be killed like the lady was in Psycho. Okay, so she was in the shower but the idea is the same.

It does not take long for me to settle in our temporary home. He is going to talk with the fellows. I take the time to check my e-mail on my cool ass brand spanking new phone. Nothing is there except something from May about needing a sitter when I get back.

I think about calling Robert. I discard the idea. I am having way too much fun. I get in my warm but sexy nightie then crawl under the sheet for some rest. I deserve a quick nap. Being in constant movement can be a bit wearing on the body.

Sleep beckons then overtakes me. I don't know how long I sleep until a knock at the door wakes me from my slumber. A quick look around shows Mr. M.O.P. has not returned. I may as well answer it, since he is still with the fellows. I feel no hesitancy. It is probably only the housekeeping staff to clean.

***

Meet Alita

There is a tall, as in bigger than me, woman on the other side of the door. She does not have a cart with soap, lotion and towels with her. Maybe she is lost.

"Yes, can I help you?"

"You must be Lynn," she says in a voice full of confidence.

Hmm, I am not getting a good feeling about this. I say, "Yes? Can I help you?"

"I am Alita, his wife," she says gracefully commanding respect.

Oh, shit. This can't be good. I mean, I knew he had a wife. Over there. Somewhere. Certainly not here at our, no, his, hotel room. Why the hell does she know my name? That damn Marty. He probably called her just to come and kill me.

Who forgot to send out the cheating memo that says wives and girlfriends should not be in the same room? Well, I am technically not his girlfriend. We have not slept together, like that, slept together. Heavy kissing where bodily fluids have almost been released does not count, does it?

Okay, let me think about weapons at my disposal. There is a corkscrew on the counter in the mini-kitchen. I need to get to it. If she tries anything, I am going for her throat. Cock-sucking son of a bitch. My cursing lessons have come to the fore. Kiss my ass.

How am I going to explain the headlines "Woman Kills Man's Wife, and then Waits in His Hotel Room with her Dead Body and Kills Him?" I'll plead insanity like the woman that killed her kids. I need a damn good attorney for this. I wonder if my attorney friend Dottie does double murder cases. In Tennessee.

Maybe I should also kill myself. No. I don't want to die. Life ain't real good right now, but it could turn around. If I can get out of this shit, I am going home. I am never going anywhere but to work anymore. And, maybe to my kids house every now and again.

Oh, and if I get the chance to go to Lima, Peru, I will. Okay, stop brain. Here is the wife of the man that I have been enjoying, learning, and wanting in the room with me. What the fuck? So my brain just up and leaves my mind a total blank. I am left to fend for myself.

"Would you like to come in?"

Could I keep her out? If it were my husband's hotel room, I would be sooo in there.

"Yes, I am here at his request. He wanted us to meet."

She has such a fascinating accent. Is she stunning? Hell yes. She is so chocolate; her name should have been Ebony. Her skin is clear and unnaturally smooth. Maybe the texture is the result of using the blood of the women who had intruded on her man to cleanse her face and hands.

She is somewhere between 35 and 55. Her double D's make my single B's look anorexic. Damn, I should have gotten some breast implants with my last tax refund. At least then, I would have more confidence, the way generously endowed women do.

If I get out of this, I am buying myself some titties. I will throw them out on the table at meetings and have them on display even in the winter. I will dare people to stare at them. But I have to get out of this shit first. My attention goes back to the one hundred fifty pound woman in the room.

Her dress is a flowing number that matches her exotic looks. A lush color that may be purple. You could just as easily call this color blue. Even flowing, it does not hide her full shape. Like him, she exudes an energy that mere mortals can't ignore. She talks with her hands. She is gesturing like a graceful window washer. Her voice sounds like an Eartha Kitt purr. She stands about five nine in her stocking feet. On this occasion, a pair of gold stiletto heels, that add at least five inches, encase her feet.

"I've just got here from Paris. I will be leaving tonight."

I know she is here to kill me. Then she will catch the next flight out. I have to make sure I have her DNA under my nails before she does me in so the police will have a clue. I find myself mesmerized by her gestures, caught up in her ability to shrink the room. Well, maybe I am shrinking myself. She and her husband are master mesmerists.

If I can get to my purse, I could get out of here and catch the next plane smoking, to a safe place. Home. Wait a minute. Did she just say that he wants us to meet? Okay, act cool, like I have been in hotel rooms with married men, when their wives show up invited by him. What is really going on here?

She comes in the room as if she paid for it. Along with her comes more excitement than I have seen in the past sixteen years. She is Grace Jones strong. She smokes cigarettes and probably other plants. I smell the scent as she passes.

She is barely in the door before she asks me, "Do you mind if I smoke?"

However, it is a rhetorical question since she has already lit up by the time the question clears her lips. She has a gold cigarette holder that appears from nowhere and is an extension of her fingers. Her fingers look like she should be a hand model. But then you would miss the rest of her. She is such a total package, just seeing her hands would be a travesty. As she speaks smoke wafts up around her head lending an eerie quality to her words.

Her hair is in dreads, longer than my twists, down her back. They are thick as cigars. Every finger has a ring on it. They are gold rings with colored stones on one hand and silver with colored stones on the other. There are silver bracelets on one arm, and gold on the other. The constant movement of her hands causes her sleeves, scarves, and everything about her to be in constant motion, billowing, adding flavor, emphasis, punctuation and visuals to her words. She captivates, as does he. They belong together.

"He asked me to come, to give my approval," she states as she allows the couch to touch her body. The couch coos.

"Approval for what" I ask in my firm voice still standing, still alert and ready for battle.

"Well, he told me he had met a woman on the plane that he was enchanted with. Generally, it is not important enough for him to tell me of these erotic interludes. Frankly, there have not been many women that he sees. In his business, the opportunity to sample variety is great. He does not partake, preferring to keep himself above the physical. But for some reason, you are one that he believes is a past life."

"What the hell are you talking about? What do you mean past life? We have shared conversation, shared a hotel room, but we have not been intimate."

That was really a balm to my conscience. If he had made the effort or if I was not such a wimp, we would have been doing so much more by now.

"For him, it is more than that. If you would be honest with me, you would admit it is also that way for you. I noticed the way you greeted me at the door. Your response, when I told you I was his wife, was a fear that I was here as the jealous wife. But, I assure you that is not the case. I have no reason to be jealous." She smiles and reaches out to touch my arm.

She is so right. She makes me wonder why he is wasting time with me when he has her at home. This woman is totally captivating. Her voice gives me comfort without her making the effort. I find myself wanting to open up to her, share with her and for her to understand what I am doing in a hotel room in Nashville. With her husband. However, I have nothing to say. How could I explain what I don't understand?

Her words weave a connection between us. "So, you met him on the plane. Tell me about when you felt the attraction."

I do, leaving nothing out and ending with an apology for any distress that I may have caused her. Because I need to, I tell her that nothing has happened, but not because of a lack of desire on my part.

"He was waiting for me to come and he is right to do so," is her response.

This is starting to sound freaky. I am not into threesomes I think. However, I've never been in one. It may be speculation on my part.

"Tell me what you feel when you are with him. Does he excite you? He must, since you have taken time out of your life to be here," she says in that throaty voice of hers.

Again, I tell her everything, leaving nothing out. She seems like such an understanding ear.

"I desire him. I want there to be something, but I don't know what. I dream of him. I feel him, even if we are not speaking, just being in the same space creates a physical something that is more than lust. I really can't explain it."

The chair lets me flop into it without telling me to get up and let it experience her. I could tell the chair was jealous of the couch.

"It seems that I was right to come so quickly" are the words that flow from her throat as her lips curve into a smile.

Of course, I ask the obvious question. "Why?"

"Well, it is not simply a case of mere wanting on a physical level. What makes this different is the intensity of the emotions that you are feeling. He recognizes that what is happening is more than physical. He wants to have you prepared properly?"

Again, I question her, "Prepared for what?"

"Are you familiar with the concept of the elusive orgasm," she asks me.

"What? No, I am sure I get mine so there is nothing elusive in that. Since you bring it up, if I could get with him one time, I'd be over this infatuation. At least I hope I would be over this strangeness," I tell her.

She laughs, and the sound is so melodic, she could have been singing. Then she starts to explain. "People say that there are times when there is a release that can be achieved on three levels. The physical, the mental, and the spiritual," she ticks off holding up the required number of fingers on her perfectly manicured hand. "With certain people, there is a connection on all of the levels. This is when the elusive orgasm occurs."

She continues, "Some people never experience this melding, others may once in a lifetime. The belief is these three sides are connected and when you meet one that causes the strong attraction on all levels, it results in the completeness of the orgasm. If you don't have this total connection, the lack does not stop you from finding release on other levels. However, you don't complete the release to its fullness, it remains elusive," she purrs.

"Physical release is easy to achieve. There need not be effort made to secure this temporal satisfaction. When you meet one who can secure the release on a mental level, you can share ideas in addition to the physical release. You can converse without words. When you meet one that you connect to spiritually, something inside of one reaches out to envelop the reaching out and being enveloped by the other.

But the one who can connect physically, spiritually and mentally, this is who has the key to the total, complete, elusive, orgasm. Then you find true release." Her explanation of an elusive orgasm causes a definite excitement in me.

She continues, "While it is physically felt, it is not lust. The souls will enter and be entered respectively. This is when the elusive orgasm occurs, the true petit mort, which the French know and understand. When you find this person, be careful. They can alter your life.

Americans call it a chemical attraction but they are wrong. It is more. It is souls joining again over time and past lives. "It makes you crazy. You stalk to catch a glimpse of that person. You call just to hear their voice. Your mood swings in relationship to where you are with the other person. Once you have unleashed that energy, the power builds again. That is what you are feeling for him, and he for you," she says.

I think she is right. I wait for her to continue.

"I will allow this to occur. I will share him with you for the time that he is here, but you must not come to him in Paris. Your space with him is here. We will be mates for this time, this space. I will not come back to the States without your permission during your time together."

Is she saying I can sleep with her husband? That is what I am hearing.

"I should tell you to run away from this feeling, but the fantasy would be forever. You would then spend your life dreaming about what could, what might have been. Better that you live it and have the completion of the experience again," she concludes. I am in stunned silence. "Now come, I will prepare you for him as I will prepare him for you," she states.

She has not raised her voice but I feel the command and start to respond to her instructions.

However, I have to ask her, "How can you put up with this? Knowing that he is cheating on you, that he isn't faithful?"

"Oh ma chere, he isn't cheating on me. My eyes are not closed. This, what is flowing between the two of you does not diminish what he and I have together."

"Don't you want him to be with only you? I wouldn't want my husband to be with anyone else," I tell her.

"No. I want him to live. I want him to be free to share any thoughts with me as I feel that freedom with him. I don't want him constricted, restrained, or repressed. An unlived fantasy is a dangerous thing. It is a ghost that can't be faced because it shifts, changes, always being better than reality. Then there is the trust. I trust him completely," she states with the conviction of the secure.

"How can you when you know that he has been with others?" I don't understand her.

"I trust him not to be loose. I trust him to seek more than physical release. He also trusts me to do the same. Thus, we have strengthened our love and commitment to each other, in the open. We don't hide, nor are we ashamed.

We recognize complete attraction that is deeper than a physical release. Our years together have been magical, even if there are no more," she gives a shrug that says more than words. "It just is what we have. I will not miss what I can't measure. I can't measure love."

"Has he ever prepared you?" I ask to satisfy my curiosity.

"Tell me how the answer to that question will change your life?" she asks with a smile. "But I will answer you. Yes, he has. I lived it, welcomed it, as I welcome your involvement in his life at this time. So what will you decide?"

The door opening announces his entrance. Both of us turn to look at him. She from her space on the couch, me from the chair beside her. He comes towards us in the sitting area. He acknowledges me with a smile before saying "hello," in that sexy ass voice of his. Even though his wife is sitting right there, I can't help but to smile in return. He is not in the least awkward, embarrassed, or nervous.

She levitates off the couch so he can envelope her in a hug that I want to be mine. She is so fucking graceful. Where do you go to learn that?

"Beloved," she utters by way of greeting.

Who in the hell says that shit in real life and makes it seem normal? Wait one minute; I am the one here in a hotel room in Nashville with her husband. Maybe I shouldn't be so critical.

I am beginning to feel inferior. When he and I were here, alone, I was fine. Seeing them together is sobering. Hell, I am not even into women, and I would want her. I guess I am turning lesbian. That will go over very well. I'll open "Ms. Lynn's Home for Imaginary Lesbians." It will be for women who are attracted to their almost, but not quite, boyfriends' wives. But what will I do with Robert? I don't know. I'll think about that later.

He kisses her on the cheek, which she accepts with more of the grace that she should bottle to sell.

"I'm glad you made it so soon," he tells her.

I feel like a spectator in someone else's living room. They are holding hands while standing in front of the couch. The love flowing between them is apparent. They are made for each other, each with their own exotic beauty. There is no distinction between the two. They have an aura that surrounds them. It makes them appear as one.

I need to go home. Maybe I can slip out without being missed. No sooner did I have the thought than they turn to me as one. They invite me into what would now be a group hug. I enter their oneness. Damn, it feels good.

As we are having this group hug, he speaks. "This is why we were waiting," he tells me. "Alita is my wife."

No shit Sherlock I think. I say, "I know she told me everything."

"Will you allow her to prepare us for this?" He asks me this as he has one arm around her and one arm around me.

"Yes." I answer him as I have one arm around him and one arm around his wife. This is just a bit odd.

Alita smiles. She takes my hand as she breaks our touchy feely time. She stops long enough to pick up a small bag by the couch that I don't even remember seeing her bring in. She leads me into the bathroom and turns on the bright lights.

I feel his presence before I see his reflection in the mirror. Now the reflection in the mirror shows three faces, all three pairs of eyes in the mirror are looking at me. Talk about putting it all out there.

"Please remove your gown," Alita says.

I do, aware that this is the first time he has seen me naked. My inferiority grows by leaps and bounds, as my breasts appear to shrivel like man parts in cold water. They seem to want to meet my back to tell some secret. Since they were never impressive, this is mortifying.

Alita gathers one in her palm." You have nursed," she observes.

"Yes, three times. I think my children ate all of the good parts then left the skin," I confess.

She smiles, as does he. Alita gathers the other breast in her hand and kisses the top of each one. She unzips a small bag I did not even see her with and lays out a razor, followed by a dish with some type of soap on it. She partially fills the dish with warm water.

"First, I will remove your hair." It does not seem like a good idea, letting this woman remove hair from my body with a razor. I am looking at them both in the mirror. Alita hugs me protectively and warmly. She says, "Don't be afraid, no harm will come to you."

I am watching him. His voice is impassive. He says, "Whatever you want to happen will happen. You may stop this at anytime." His eyes are speaking volumes saying, "Trust." I think about that for about a minute. During that time, neither of them moves. I think about her telling me of the trust she has in him.

"Go ahead," I tell her.

She smiles as she lifts my left arm. She works the soap and water into lather. I have never smelled such a scent before. It has a fruity sweetness, with a hard underlying strength that defies my attempts at description. It stays in the nostrils without intruding or irritating. It smells like a blend of flowers and a type of musk. It definitely is not chamomile. But hell, I can't tell chamomile from hydro. She makes quick work of shaving under first one then the other arm.

Alita turns to him and has him remove all of his clothing. She rubs the lather into his right arm. With the same amount of tenderness, she clears his underarm of hair. Lifting his left arm, she repeats the ritual.

When our underarms are free of hair, she rinses off all soap residue. Then she takes one hand from both of us and leads us out of the bathroom and into the bedroom. Once there she lays us onto the bed side by side facing the mirror on the closet door. She goes back to retrieve the soap and razor. We look at each other.

"Are you sure," he asks me.

I can only nod. He takes my hand as we wait for Alita to come back into the room where we are laying.

When Alita comes back, she exudes some of the excitement we feel. She starts with him this time. Her smile is infectious as she lifts his sex to begin shaving. Boy did he grow. As she kneels to shave him, he gets even harder. He looks like so much delicious, I don't know how she keeps from slipping her lips around him. He definitely needs extra large condoms.

I watch because I don't want to miss a thing. He watches me, watching him. It is too exciting to turn my head away. Once hair removal has been completed, Alita smiles. She wipes the lather on a towel she has laid between us.

Now it is my turn. Alita works up a nice lather in her hands. She works the lather gently but firmly into my pubic hairs. I have never had a woman touch me, there, that I could remember. I want to believe it is just because I am horny that I am so turned on right now. It can't be because a woman has her hands on my … Yea, I will go with that. I question my sexuality again before deciding it does not really matter. Whatever it is, I'm in for it.

I am as smooth as a nectarine when she is finished. She runs hands over both of us to make sure she has not missed anything. Then it is back to the bathroom where we stand in front of the mirror.

Alita looks at us both before she begins to speak. She pulls long gold chains from somewhere. The gold is so delicate the chains look like strands of hair braided together to make something the size of a strand of angel hair pasta. It can't possibly stand pressure. It is much too delicate, barely discernable to the eye.

"Imagine an invisible bond like this golden chain that I will use to encircle your waist."

She puts a chain around my waist. She fastens it in the back. "This is your spiritual self, where you exist, the part of you that transcends all time. How does it feel?"

It is a snug fit, enough room to breathe, not binding or tight. The chain is feather light. I can feel it enough to know that it is there, but not restrictive.

"I feel safe," I reply.

She slips the chain around his waist while still talking. "Some people connect repeatedly over time and lifetimes. Their recognition of each other from their past lives occurs on a spiritual level. It is that feeling of having known someone forever when you first meet." She looks into his eyes to gently whisper, "How do you feel?"

"I accept this," he says.

I look at him, wanting to ask what he is accepting. I decide instead to continue to watch the ceremony go forward.

Alita continues with him. Lifting another chain, she begins fastening it to the chain at his waist in the back. She brings the other end down his ass then up between his thighs. In the front, she wraps it around his shaft. His shaft is standing at attention to make sure all eyes can see its impressive length and width. She connects it to the chain at his waist in the front, all the time talking.

"Your physical self is often satisfied. You are used to operating on this level. The physical release is common, it does not require thought or even attraction. However, it is superficial by itself. This is what animals have, the blind lust. How does it feel," she asks him.

"I am ready," is his reply. Yep. He looks ready to me.

She turns to me. As she is working, she keeps the conversation going. Talk about a mind fuck.

"Physical sex can be enjoyable. However, it is fleeting, quickly forgotten."

She is behind me attaching another chain in the back to the one at my waist. Then parting my rear cheeks she brings the chain down and back up to the front, parting all flesh as she goes. I am trying extremely hard to stay focused.

Again, she connects the chain in the front before asking, "How does it feel?"

"I don't know." I don't want to say, "Do you see my nipples puckering?"

Slight movements let me know the chains are there. It is very sensual feeling something so light and exquisite in my private space. Our eyes meet in the mirror. She smiles. That's right. He had prepared her before. She knows exactly how I am feeling.

"I feel excited," I confess.

"Most of the time, you connect with people on one maybe two levels, either deeply or lightly."

As she continues to explain, her hands are creating an erotic sensation. The touches on my body are robbing me of thought, starting an inner heat. She wraps another chain around my head like some type of flower child from the sixties.

"A mental attraction is more lasting, to know another, share thoughts, that is to be desired."

She is weaving her own spell. Her words enthrall me. She attaches the chain in the back of my head before applying a final chain that attaches the one at my head to the one at my waist, going down my back.

Again, she asks the question, "How does it feel?"

I recognize the rightness of the question. I bask in the beauty of the ceremony, her words, everything. I think for a moment and respond, "It feels right."

As she works with him, I continue to watch. Her hands on him are sure, not hesitant. I envy her the balls to be so bold. He is watching me in the mirror as she encircles his head with the matching chain.

"For the mind to accept the mental orgasm, it must be unafraid. Trust is key, knowledge that the giving, the receiving, is wanted and returned," she explains. When she finishes, she asks her standard question.

He gives the same answer. "I am ready."

We return to the bed. There he tells me she will rub oil into both of us as we lay beside each other. She takes the oil out.

He stops her asking, "Are you sure?"

"Yessss," is her response.

The whole thing is strange. I make a mental note to ask him about it later. The scent of the oil, like the soap, is not familiar.

Alita begins with me. "Please lie face down."

I turn for her to pour this warm (when did she heat it?) oil into my back. With my arms at my sides, she starts in my head, blending this oil into my hair and scalp. She is kneading the muscles at my neck and shoulders. They part and relax for her, as do my legs. She is not in a rush.

"The oil is for your senses. The smell allows your internal self to join in the sensations that the rest of your body is feeling."

She touches every part of the back of me. The oil is not just on the surface. She massages it into my body, soul and spirit. As she strokes the back of my legs, I wish she would stay. The oil is soothing and electrifying.

Once she finishes with my back she says, "I am ready for you to turn onto your back."

Then she starts on my front. She works the oil into my face stroking my eyebrows, hairline and lips.

"The openings in your face are all connected. Taste mingles with smell, enhanced by the eye."

Even my ears don't escape her notice. She proceeds to pour oil onto my breasts. She strokes them enough to make me think I was a D-cup. She holds them, lets the warmth from her fingers encase them and make them feel significant. I watch her and want to speak but can't. She continues to stroke over my abdomen, astounding me and almost taking my breath away with her firmness.

Alita moves to do the front of my legs. She spreads my legs open then put oil in all of my secret places, rubbing briskly then softly. Then she is finished with me. I am not sure how I feel about that.

Alita kisses me on my lips then turns to him to say, "You have chosen well." I try not to think.

I watch her start to massage him. He is on his stomach. If I could record this, it would sell like hotcakes. He watches me.

"The warmth of the oil will limber your muscles. You will have a greater freedom of movement," Alita explains.

As he turns for her to do the important parts, I want to be the oil, a part of her on him. How she manages to keep from mounting him I don't know. I want to take the oil, stroke him and absorb him while I did. Hell, she has probably done all of that and more. She is his wife after all.

Afterwards, we stand while she dresses us in matching fabric. His pants tie in the front and back. A large dashiki completes his ensemble. My outfit wraps around my waist then goes over my head. Alita assists me to put my arms through armholes, and my head through the head hole. I doubt I could get into this thing myself.

"What about underwear," I ask.

"After tonight you will only wear a brassiere if you think it is necessary, but never panties. Likewise, he will not wear anything that would keep you from him. You will be ready for each other at all times, without barriers. Now I must leave. My work is done and you have a full night ahead. I have a flight to catch in the morning. I must be back in New York tonight." She turns to him to say "Beloved, enjoy." To me she smiles and says, "Trust." Moving like ripples on water, she gathers her things.

As we walk her to the door and down to the lobby, I am still trying to make sense of it all. She had arranged to take the shuttle back to the airport. She turns to kiss him goodbye. I must have looked wistful because she turns and kisses me too.

It is now thirty minutes to lobby call. He goes back to the room to grab his drum bag. I don't want to go back to the room. I feel as though every nerve ending is exposed, waiting. I need to be with him in unhurried moments. I need to end this anticipation. I need the completeness. I wait in the lobby. As the fellows come down, there are a few comments and questions.

"You met Alita," asks Marty.

"Yes," I answer him. I finally receive a smile.

"You are the mate," asks Shaun

"No. What is a mate," I ask him.

"When a man has more than one woman, not a mistress, but another woman that is not hidden but in the open, then they are mates if his wife accepts," he tells me.

"Well then, yes," I again respond.

"I'm not surprised," comes from Willie.

"By any chance do you have a sister, cousin, or daughter that you would like me to meet since you are off limits," is Leon's contribution.

"No," is my negative to him and we all laugh.

Mr. M.O.P. comes back down ready for the gig. We pile in for the ride. The venue is the Grand Old Opry. I'm surprised. They are definitely not country. They are a part of a highly publicized show with incredibly diverse music offerings. Once there I go to our assigned seats while they go backstage.

I am sitting a seat away from Jill Scott then see Gretchen Wilson further up front. It would be bad form to shout out "Hey Jill, Gretch, what's up? Do you remember me? I brought all of your music?" I resist the temptation but I love their music.

They are the fifth act on stage. It is a different sound from when they were at the club in Cleveland. I don't like it as much because there are so many people, the music lacks the intimacy of that night. I can't see them clearly, because they are so far away.

The sound comes through loud and clear. It is on point but I prefer cozy. Once their set is over, they come to the audience for the remainder of the show. VH1 is taping the show for a special. They will air it in the next few weeks. No one I know would be watching it so I feel secure in enjoying myself. Besides, even if they saw me on television, no one would believe that I went to the Grand Old Opry.

The show finishes about one in the morning. The ride back to the hotel has a different kind of energy. If knowing there has been sexual tension before, and there had been, returning to the hotel room from the gig is different. Like heat from the last drop of water that burns out of the pan before the fire starts. I can barely sit. I know the others in the band can see the smoke drifting up from between my legs. Nobody speaks. I have never felt so much like a nymphomaniac.

Even though I am just sitting in my seat, trying to look out of the window, at other people, at anywhere and anybody but him, I feel him. I try to ignore him. It doesn't work. Every time I glance his way, he is looking at me. It reminds me of our time on the plane, only ten times more concentrated. I don't know how we survive the ride. Once at the hotel, we say our goodnights. Since today is to be a free day, we chat about plans before drifting, or in our case running off to our respective rooms.

He is frightening. The intensity should have been a sign for me to run while I still could. However, from the day that I chose to run away, it was too late. I am prepared, maybe physically but in no way mentally.

Once inside the room, it is time for the completion. As soon as the door closes behind me, he grabs my arm and puts my back to the door. Our previous kisses elicited a sensual reaction. They did not prepare me for this raw, intense, onslaught. Rational thought intrudes. I may not be ready to have someone inside me.

We have to stop. It has been over twenty-seven years of fidelity. Am I ready to give this up? I must be. Something deep in my mind or in my body holds me here. It is not going to allow me to leave without the experience of being sexually here with him on all levels.

I understand completely what Alita was saying. It put into words how I feel when I am with him. Our previous conversations and time together is a prelude to what is about to happen. This is the opportunity to be truly complete.

He dominates me. I want to run away because I feel so on edge and skittish. It is just too much. My mind, my body can't take it all at this time. I need to separate these feelings somehow, so it is not all enveloping me at once. When he questions me with a look, I am saying no and yes and everything and nothing. I am trying to buy time, to stop the act from being completed. He is relentless, following, pulling, tugging, but always leaving space for me to make the final decision.

His tongue in my mouth holds me hostage, as my body surges forward then away from his. I notice a furtive movement. I am stunned to see my left leg hanging over his right arm where his hand and body are pinning me to the wall. Am I standing on one leg in a three-inch stiletto? I must be.

I could not move if I wanted to because he is standing between my legs. The image in the mirror is so erotic I have to close my eyes to keep my sanity. I must be suffering from the Stockholm syndrome, because I don't really want to leave. I want to stay and feel him inside me.

I get a prelude. He pulls, parts, and penetrates me so quickly it takes a moment for me to realize that my orgasm is dripping into his hand. This easy access outfit of Alita's is a wonderful thing. We are now moving around the wall taking turns being against the wall as we struggle for domination.

The couch interrupts as we stumble over it. We both stop to take stock of where we are and what is coming next.

Somehow, I get my arm and head out of the holes of my outfit. I hurriedly take off my shoes before I break something. He makes quick work of shedding his apparel.

We get to the bed. And then he fucks me. No slow motion gauzy romanticism, no euphemisms. He fucks me in real time and it is stunning. There are gentler words to describe the experience, but I don't think they would capture the flavor of what I feel. His hands alternate between my waist, head and between my legs. The gold chains on us only add to the sensations.

He has both of his hands on my head, pulling this chain, squeezing my head, pushing and pulling at the same time. All the time, he is over me, fucking me. Then he is at my waist, squeezing, kneading. Yes, he is fucking me. Between my legs, he is playing me like one of his instruments. The tapping on my nether region, reminds me of the gig we had just left. He is playing me. I don't know the notes just the sensation. And he is fucking me.

His hands on my waist tighten as if I am a talking drum. His arm is around me with just the right amount of pressure to make me give him the orgasm my body has waiting for him. And he is still fucking me. My head feels like he is playing the conga on it, both hands. He is manipulating the skin and scalp, alternately tapping and stopping the vibration.

Between my legs, he is playing the instrument with the beads, pulling and shaking and stroking with fingers that have had way too much experience touching and stroking skin and a body that is content to continue fucking me. The sounds and sensations of the chains connecting between us, on us, open up another avenue for release.

And we ignite the scent, the oil that Alita had massaged into us, by joining and heating the oil, causing my whole body to feel warm. It releases a smell that touches my olfactory senses and they explode into their own orgasm. My eyes are open, but I can't see a damn thing. This man is fucking me so tough; I can't make a sound or form a thought.

This is way too much pleasure to take in at one time. And the momentum continues to build, and he is going faster and I am joining him faster. And then I shatter crying out because of the beauty of it all. And then he shatters, crying out my name and holding me tightly as I am holding him.

I am afraid now it is over. It is as extraordinary as I expected, remembered, or dreamed it would be. Then he, or I, spoil it with spurious words of love that I am not naïve enough to buy into I tell myself. We can't love each other. We don't know each other. However, it is more than lust. I wish I knew what it is.

Our bodies are still joined and we are still connecting too much for my sanity. This is not a love affair. I don't know what it is. I chose to walk away from my reality to live a two-week fantasy. It is a specified time in the span of my life. It will be ending all too soon. I have to start putting distance between us. Well, maybe not tonight. I am feeling too much to do that now. I just want to memorize him, store him up for the times I need to feel as though I am living again.

He will be my reminder that sometimes, life is good and sometimes it is damn good. So here is a memory for my memory box. I know that time and reality is the enemy.

I want to believe this thing could burn itself out if time would slow and reality would intrude.

We have nothing in common. In the normal course of things, we would have never met. Damn plane ride. Would I have missed this experience if I could? I would not have wanted too. In many ways, it has been an epiphany, a tap on the shoulder, a yell to start living again.

I don't want to be sad when this is over, but I do want a clean break. No looking back. No regrets. I am a big girl. I can do this. It is absolutely amazing how quickly you become attuned to someone's voice, touch, and presence. I hope the opposite is also true. I know if I were Alita, I would not think about anyone else. I would just want him to think about me.

That night we sleep in each other's arms. We wake up the same way. More loving comes with the daylight. Tender this time but every bit as satisfactory.

***

Jack Daniels Live

I feel awkward along with being a tad bit sore getting up the next morning. What do you say to someone you meet and decide to run away with for two weeks? Then you meet his wife who tells you an erotic story and prepares you to sleep with her husband. Then you have fantastic sex with him? I decide to concentrate on what I will wear to the distillery instead. I wonder if he feels as content and as sexually satisfied as I feel right now.

Finding Passion: Confessions of a Fifty Year Old Runaway

I put on a mid-length blue fishtail skirt with a pink
blouse and declare myself ready. Then I wake him up. He
asks me if I want to talk. I don't. He takes the opportunity
to get dressed. I take the opportunity to practice not being
embarrassed by waking up with a stranger I feel I have
known forever. He decides to wear black slacks with a gold
polo shirt. We head to the lobby to wait for the tour bus to
come. I am not particularly fond of whiskey, but it is what
they do in Tennessee.

He shares that he has a passing acquaintance with the
beverage, but the rudiments of whiskey making have
eluded him thus far. I am glad to have a hand in his
educational process. The bus is here promptly at ten. On
the ride down, we hold hands. I sure do like the touching.
There are three other pick-ups. The driver announces on the
speaker we should sit back and enjoy the ride.

I am sure I will, I don't need to be told. He informs us
we should arrive at the distillery by 1:30. On the ride, I
think of how I can work this tourist attraction into a
conversation at work or with friends. I remember that it
can't be a part of any conversation because technically I am
not supposed to be here. Just the same, I am heading off to
Lynchburg with a man I met on a plane.

Hell of a name for a city, I hope the residents don't take
the town name literally. I can see the headlines now on the
front page. It will say, "Musician and his Consort Lynched
in Lynchburg." Wait, only kings and queens have consorts.
Maybe it will say, "Man and Woman Found Hanging in
Lynchburg," under the fold on the first page. Hmmm, he is
not that famous. We may get, "Two People Dead in the
City," on page B3. However, we are black and we are in
the south, so it will most likely read, "We Got Two More,"

at the end of the "Looking to Buy" section on page F46, under the fold.

Once at the distillery, we get out and go into the welcome area. There is a pasty white statue of Jack Daniels that confronts us as we get off the bus. I have my camera and convince him to take a picture with Jack. He agrees but only if we take one together. Of course, someone agrees to his request to take our picture if we will return the favor. So we pose on either side of Jack to have our moment with a statue immortalized. We then sit in the welcome area where we learn more than we want to know about Jack from a video the distillery shows before the tour.

We are part of tour group number eight. They tell us to stay with our tour. They call our tour group number after about five minutes. Our tour guide is Rusty who can trace his ancestry back to Jack himself. He has on overalls, a white tee shirt, and some boots topped off with a baseball cap. Rusty has a southern drawl that sounds like a foreign language. He prepares us to absorb all he knows about Jack.

We get on a bus to go over to the rick yard, a new word for my vocabulary, where they make the charcoal. All Jack Daniels whiskey goes through a charcoal filter process. They only use maple wood to make the charcoal. Rusty says it gives the whiskey the right taste. I never knew that they actually poured it over charcoal. It takes the whiskey one and a half days to make it through the charcoal journey.

In order to be Tennessee Whiskey, the distillery must pour the whiskey over the charcoal in Tennessee. For the Gentleman Jack, the whiskey goes through the charcoal twice. It comes out smoother, whatever that means. This is an enlightening experience already. They use rye, corn, and barley malt to make the mash that eventually makes the whiskey. It takes five gallons of mash to make one gallon of whiskey. At the fermenter room, we see where the grains enter the process.

It's a good thing I'm wearing comfortable shoes because the stairs are something to endure. We are climbing up and down flights to follow the path of the whiskey. Mr. M.O.P. seems to be dragging at the last set of stairs to the top. He must be tired. Ahead of him, I am trying to keep up with the rest of the group. His hand in mine slows me down. Under my cute skirt, I feel the telltale feel of his hand on my tail making its way to my bottom set of lips.

I am wearing the chains around my waist and between my legs. Nothing else is there except his hand. If a strong wind comes, Jack's tourists will see a whole lot of me. I slow down so that I can get the full effect of his hands. I forget to be indignant. When I look at him, he has that oh so innocent smile that might fool someone but not me.

"Pay attention," I hiss, semi-aroused.

We get to the top and hear Rusty expounding on the fermenting process where mash turns sour. Everyone has the opportunity to smell the aroma of the sour mash. It smells as appetizing as it sounds.

He incorrigibly lifts his hand to his nose and loudly inhales. I know the scent that is going in his nose. Lord please, don't let me be dripping sex juice in Jack Daniels distillery. He winks. I check my legs for a drizzle. It's all clear. I make a dignified turn to follow the tour group down more stairs then outside to Jack's spring.

The day is hot and so am I. Thankfully, there is a cool breeze. It is coming from the cave located at the base of a mountain where the water, originally used for the whiskey, flows. Hopefully some cool air will calm me down.

There is another statue of Jack and we get on either side of him and have our picture taken, hugging Jack and each other. Then I notice the trees look strange. They have something spongy and black on them. It covers the tree limbs but not the leaves. I ask Rusty about it.

Rusty shares that revenuers used trees as a sign during the prohibition period. The trees served as a sign to law enforcement that moonshine was being made in the vicinity. The process of whiskey making causes mold to cover surrounding trees.

Frankly, I am quickly losing interest in the tour. I would rather be back at the hotel finishing what Mr. M.O.P. started. I persevere through Jack's house and the safe that led to his ultimate demise. It would have been more appropriate if Jack had gotten drunk and fell into his spring.

Instead, he died because he kicked his safe. That kick caused an infection in Jack's foot. The infection became fatal. I would have expected a more exciting ending.

We trudge onward, through the pictures of Jack's descendents, the barrels (that can only be used three times before they are useless to the barrelhouse), through the hand bottled whiskey, and everything else. Jack Daniels makes a lot of liquor, sixteen hundred cases per day. I learn you can't tap the barrels for bottling until the whiskey taster approves the taste. What a job.

We get to have lemonade free once we get back to the welcome center. Rusty already explained to us that the county was dry. Even though the distillery makes big bucks selling liquor everywhere else, they could not sell it in Lynchburg.

The company finally received approval to sell collector whiskey bottles at the gift shop. They are happy to sell these souvenir bottles at a price higher than the whiskey sells for in the stores. Mr. M.O.P. gets us each a bottle that we can register on the Internet. This way everyone (who cares) will know that we took the tour and were suckers enough to fall for the souvenir bottle bullshit. It is a nice memory box gift though.

At the end of the tour, all tourists take the obligatory walk to Lynchburg Square. If you spend five dollars at participating merchants, you get a free shot glass. Therefore, we go over the bridge then down the way about ten minutes to see what they have to offer. The walk serves another purpose. The driver parks the bus at the end of the square. We have to walk to town to get back on the bus.

This city knows business. Antique shops, that they can accurately call junk stores, line the street on both sides. There are also original shops, some selling jewelry, others selling food, and others selling handmade knickknacks are interspersed along the avenue. We settle on caps that say, 'Do you know Jack?' in pink and blue. Then we head for the bus. Damn, we are holding hands again. Then once again, his hand is at my waist starting a steady downward slide.

We get back to the hotel in a great mood. We both decide to take a quick nap. The air conditioning in the hotel is welcome after the day in the sun. Once in bed, we both also decide to make sure all sexual parts are still working. Alcohol fumes may have affected something. Slow and easy, quite different from the mutual attack of last night. We drift into a well-laid sleep, the kind where your body is floating. We are still holding each other.

The phone wakes us up two hours later. The fellows want to know if we want to go to dinner. To save time we decide to shower together. In the interest of being helpful, he offers to wash my back if I will wash his. He designs his movements to arouse me and they do. I like the way the soap makes his hands glide over my skin. When it is my turn to return the favor, I take my time to make sure I am doing a thorough job.

The feel of the water distracts us. I have my back to the water to rinse off. He is behind me. I feel his hand caressing my ass before slipping around my waist and down to play on my lips. Of course, I had to grant him an all access pass, so I open my legs to his fingers. He allows one to slip inside of me. I lean against the wall because he is playing me again.

Stroking, rubbing, creating the sensation. The placement of my foot on the side of the tub, allows him even greater access. That is when he enters me fully. I hold onto the wall to keep from falling. Sex should not be this amazing. The water covering and falling on us is an added pleasure. I don't want this to end is my thought before I have an orgasm that is anything but elusive.

Finding Passion: Confessions of a Fifty Year Old Runaway

Once out of the shower, I ask him "Will you tell me something about you that most people don't know?" He is putting the conditioner into his hair while I watch. I am becoming addicted to watching his hands.

He smiles his slow sexy smile and thinks for a moment before answering. "Most people don't know I left my country at a very young age. I have been on my own since I was fifteen," he shares.

"I did a variety of jobs as I went around the States and Europe before settling in France. I have always felt a connection to music. I used to lie about my age so I could work with different artists. Being so young, so far away from home, I grew up fast. I had to learn to care for myself. The life I lived helped to make a man of me."

I think this explains his confidence. We finish dressing, me in a nice dress (again sans pantyhose), him in khakis and a green silk shirt. Down in the lobby we start the stroll to a restaurant in the mall close to the hotel. The food is fair but the conversation is lively.

The fellows talk about different cities they have visited in the U.S. Europe, and Africa. If I ever get the chance, I want to go to Africa. I want to see Africa through my own eyes then compare my impressions to the lens this group of men has me looking through.

They laugh about how different the places are from each other. Africa comprises various countries on a single continent. The fellows share the difference in food and culture around the largest continent on the planet. Some places eat rice as a staple food. Others have white sweet potatoes called yams. They know so much about their countries of origin it is amazing. I don't even know where corn grows. They also have tremendous pride for their homelands. As we eat, the fellows continue to debate current politics and issues.

I have my horizon broadened. I must admit to cultural ignorance. I knew a man in college that was from Liberia. He only associated with other Liberians. Other African Americans used to say he thought he was better than we were.

I talked to him once or twice. I did not get that impression. I think he just did not understand why African Americans did not take more responsibility for their community and lives. He was really a flag waving Liberian. I don't know very many African Americans that have the same commitment to their country. That is sad.

After dinner, we go back to the hotel. I have to do my voice recordings before I get too far behind. While he goes and talks to the fellows, I get my diary and tape caught up by telling my recorder exactly what happened. Saying these things aloud sounds naughty, unbelievable, and stimulating. If anyone ever hears it, I will just say I made it all up. No one will believe that I can do all of these things anyway. When he gets back, we rest. The next morning we leave for Las Vegas.

***

My Travel Tips for Nashville

Visit Jack Daniels distillery even if you don't drink whiskey. And if by chance, there is ever a knock on your hotel room door, and a tall exotic looking woman is on the other side, answer it and invite her in.

TRACK FIVE: VEGAS

The flight is long but we make it to Vegas. We exit the plane and enter the airport. I am surprised. They have slot machines in the airport. Lots and lots of them. The airport is massive. By using trains, moving sidewalks and our two legs, we make it to the baggage claim area. We collect our luggage. Then we bundle into the shuttle to our destination.

We are staying at the Rio, which is a short ride from the airport. It is a beautiful place made of red and blue glass with a tropical theme. We are in Ipanema Towers. The view out of our window takes in the pool. The pool lights up at night. We can see Caesar's and Bally's, and other casinos on Las Vegas Boulevard (the Strip). The desk clerk tells me to make sure to see the Strip at night for the full effect of the lights.

Our tourist activities will include time on the Strip to get a massage. Then time downtown so we can go to Fitzgerald's and the must see Downtown attraction, the laser light show and the Fremont Street experience. An African American man owns the Fitz. I want to see it if for no other reason than to support a brother doing it in Vegas.

I put aside twenty dollars a day to gamble. If gambling starts feeling good to me, I may even spend twenty-five dollars at the one armed bandits. This is going to be a treat. Sin City watch out.

I check my e-mail. Rene has been e-mailing like crazy. I hate to admit, even to myself, that I miss my kids. I guess I have more of an attachment to my role as a mother than I have admitted.

Not surprisingly, Robert has not bothered to e-mail. Damn. Should I be hurt? Should I be angry? I wish I could work up some type of response, but what the hell. It has been over twenty-five years. Maybe Robert is feeling the same freedom as I am. He is enjoying the time that I am gone. I need to get home to put a stop to that shit. If I am not having fun, he can't be having any fun either. Oops, I forgot. I am the one that ran away and I am having a great time.

"What do you want to do first?" I inquire when we get to the room.

"How about the massage you told me about? That will remove the kinks from the flight. It will get us limber," he suggests with a smile and a step into me for a hug.

"I like the idea of getting the kinks out. Planes are really cold and drafty. The seats are too small and there is nowhere to move around without looking suspicious. Let's go for the massage." I redress in cooler pants with tennis shoes.

He, of course, is cool just as he is with a short sleeve Polo shirt and slacks.

To get to the massage spot, we will have to catch a shuttle from the Rio to the mall and then catch another shuttle from the mall to the Strip where we will have our massage.

We stand in the shade of the building while we wait and talk about the city and his previous times here. It is all amazing to me. I find the sheer size of the buildings threatening. The blue and white shuttle that the clerk said to look for arrives. Hand in hand, almost, we go to get on the shuttle.

***

Push-Ups and a Massage

Once at the mall we are outside getting our bearings to go for the massage.

He tempts me. "Since we're at the mall, let's look around," he offers.

I had spotted a little lingerie shop almost in front of where we are standing. It is calling out to me. I think this is a great idea. I should perhaps put up a token resistance. I am not a shopaholic type woman, but it is a lingerie store.

"Sure, let's go in here."

We go in. There are more undies than I would have thought possible. Crotchless panties, edible panties, and stockings with the seams in the back. But, what they have that surpasses everything else in the store is a wide selection of push-up bras, in every color of the rainbow. I have reached Nirvana.

I find a hot pink push-up bra that has matching crotchless panties. This and an electric blue push-up with the matching thong are must haves. I hold them up for his inspection. "What do you think of these?"

"I think I need to see you in them, then out of them," he tells me. He decides I also need the red corset with matching stockings. I give in graciously even though I am feeling decadent.

When we get to the counter, he stays my hand as I prepare to pay for my lingerie.

"Please, let me get this for you."

"I have money, I can afford this."

I feel slightly offended that he would try to by my underwear. Robert has never brought my underwear, and we have been together forever.

"It is not a question of if you can afford it. I want to do this. Is that wrong of me to want to buy something for you that will make me happy?"

I don't want to argue over intimates. Besides, why not accept a gift and enjoy it together? I acquiesce and he completes the purchases. It seems humorous to me that we are walking around Vegas and he is carrying a bag with a pair of thongs, a pair of crotchless panties, a corset, and some push-up bras.

We come to Caesar's Palace and admire the artwork outside, which is magnificent. The building itself is about five city blocks long and four blocks wide. We decide we may as well go inside here also. As we walk we see the ancient Roman theme is evident everywhere we look.

Busts of gladiators abound. Then there is the gambling. There are table games, slot machines, and life size statues galore. We walk around and get a feel for the place. They have a variety of restaurants and a nightclub in the building.

We come upon a shopping area inside the casino. We decide we may as well stop. I wander around and make it to the perfume counter. I decide to try on different scents. On the third sample, I come across a perfume that almost of reminds me of Alita's oil, erotic.

The name of this salute to the olfactory senses is Caesar's Woman. It would be more appropriate to call it hot sex. That is the first thing I think of when I smell it. I close my eyes on the sensation and when I open my eyes, it is to see Mr. M.O.P. standing beside me. He takes my wrist to smell what I have found.

"I would love to smell this on you. May I buy you a bottle?"

This is not a good idea. If I ever wore it, I would not be able to function. I would be too busy smelling myself. I love it.

"When I wear it I will think of you," I tell him.

"I would like that," he says with a smile and a hug for me.

It is time to leave so we can find our way to the place where we will have our massage. We take our stroll holding waist and ass as we wander out of Caesars and down the street. We find the massage parlor and go inside.

It is understated elegance with an interior decorated in warm cream paint on the walls with gold accents on the borders and molding. The plush gold furniture and gold knickknacks complete the design. This looks like a place you go to feel good. We go to the golden oak desk to check in with the receptionist.

"We would both like a massage," I tell the clerk.

She is a friendly sort and she smiles when she says, "You will love them the massages are wonderful." She checks her appointment books. "We have openings now. Would you like the massages together?" she asks.

"No," comes out in a loud squeak.

I'm shocked. I don't want anyone to see us naked together. Then I remember his wife got us naked together. Then she gave us a massage on top of that. I look at him. He is smiling as though he could see my thoughts. He gives me a slow wink before answering her question.

"We will have them separate," he tells her. "Why don't we meet at the quarter slot that was at the entry we came in when we are finished?"

"Okay, I'll see you there," I agree.

The clerk rings for two assistants. Once they materialize, she gives them instructions for us to see our separate body touchers. They lead us on our separate ways. We manage a kiss before parting.

My massage room is the size of a bedroom. It has a small table in the middle of the room. After all my travel, I am ready for an hour of pampering. There is a low chair off to the left. Beside it is a chair on wheels. I take a seat on the low chair.

"Your masseuse will be here shortly," my guide tells me with a smile. He leaves and I am left to wait.

The masseuse comes in a few minutes later. She is a short squat person. She is not exactly what I think of when I think massage. She asks about my general health and background. I know from my daughter Rene that these questions are standard. It helps to know if your massaggee is prone to heart attacks.

"Please remove everything. Then get under the sheet. I will go to allow you privacy," she barks as she turns to leave.

I have taken my clothes off for more women in the past week than I have in all my life I think as I comply with her order. I settle in under the sheet to await the removal of my kinks.

She must have been lurking around the door because as soon as I hit the massage table, she is back in. She starts some leaves growing, wind blowing, and water flowing music that is supposed to be soothing. It is not. I am lying on my back looking up at the ceiling wishing she had some Stevie Wonder, Jill Scott, or Angie Stone.

"Relax, feel the calm coming from my hands," she yaps in what I guess she thinks is a soothing voice. She sounds bored. I close my eyes waiting on her to start. Nothing happens. I peek to see what she is doing. She is standing over me waving her arms over my legs. Her eyes are also closed. Then she starts the wave up my body. Shouldn't she have her hands on me? I am not paying for a hand wave; I am paying for a massage. At about the time I am ready to ask her, "What the hell are you doing," she speaks.

She says, "I will start with your feet, which is where all your nerves end."

She flips the sheet up to my knees and proceeds to rub what I believe to be shortening into my feet. I think about the oil Alita used. Ms. Massage Lady should probably think about something lighter. She ends my foot time by pulling my second toe on each foot. My feet don't feel as relaxed as they do greasy.

She continues to grease up both my legs to my thighs. Then she greases up both arms to my shoulder. She spreads her shortening into my navel so that it can feel the horror that is occurring on other parts of my body. I am having a better understanding of how chicken wings must feel going into the deep fryer.

She has me turn over so she can grease my back. "Can you remove the chains?" she questions as she continues her lube job.

"No, they have to stay in place," I tell her.

How I am going to get them unclogged from this saturated fat is another matter. There is not much going on in the way of muscle manipulation. I feel the fat dripping as it melts off my legs and arms. If it were not for the sheet I am lying on, I would slide right off this table onto the floor.

You would not need this much grease to fry a turkey. There is now a line of her special sauce down my back. It is just waiting for me to stand up so it can run down my ass.

"Do you feel the music? Let it seep into your pores," comes from Little Ms. Mary Sunshine.

"You stopped up my pores, as well as my arteries with this lard," I think about telling her. I don't.

"Listen, you can hear the wind blowing, feel the sound of trees rustling, and a soft brook where water, the nourisher of nature is running," she screeches.

Is she serious? I feel like a smoked oyster in cottonseed oil on a winter day in Michigan and she expects me to enjoy the music. I want a bath in some nourishing water to cleanse me of the 10w40 she is caking onto me.

"I will finish with your head."

She retrieves her Crisco can from the end of the table. With a determined stride, she starts toward my twisted locks.

"No," I shout. What can I say aside from, "I am not letting you put that shit in my hair?" Think fast Lynn. "It's against my religion to have anyone touch my hair," I improvise.

"Oh, what religion is that?" she queries.

"It's a secret sect. If I told you, I'd have to kill you."

Okay, I know I am winging it. That is the best I can do verbally on short notice. Physically, I could probably take her in a fair fight, but I'm naked and greasy so she has the advantage.

She is shocked, as am I. At this point, I am willing to pay her to stop. She seems ready to leave the room immediately. I am ready for her to go.

"Oh, umm, well, ah," she stammers.

I seize my advantage. "Thank you very much. Now I have to offer prayers." I start to chant. "Whatthehellamidoinghere, whatthehellamidoinghere, whatthehellamidoinghere."

That was enough to get her out. She practically runs from the room while I'm left to ruin a perfectly good pair of flowered pants by putting them back on my trans-fat covered body. I try to use the sheet to get the majority of the excess off. The sheet must be made of Teflon because it is not absorbing anything.

I go out to the cashier where I actually pay for that death by shortening form of torture. She asks me if I want to leave a tip, which I do.

I tell her "Little Ms. Mary Sunshine needs to get some better music and a lighter oil."

I go to our designated meeting area, leaving a steady leak of oil and footprints of grease in my wake. Where is his wife when you need her?

I see him standing at the slot machine waiting for me to arrive. Not surprisingly, Mr. M.O.P. loves his massage. He does not look like someone had put the renderings of a thousand pigs into his pores. Does nothing disturb his equilibrium?

"How was your massage?" he asks.

"I've had better," is what I tell him as I think about his wife. "Why don't we head back to the hotel? That way we will not have to worry about rushing for the lobby call." I wish I didn't have to worry about becoming a human inferno when the sun ignites my fat infused self.

"Sure," he says.

We walk down to catch the shuttle back to the Rio. If he feels the grease coming out of my pants, he is too much a gentleman to mention the sensation. We make it back to the hotel and our room. It is now necessary for me to get a bath. I hope the plumbing is up to the ministrations from my masseuse. It takes four washings and five rinses before I feel clean.

It is time for him to go to rehearsal by the time I get out of the shower. The fellows will be playing tonight. "What will you do while I am at rehearsal?" he asks.

"I decided that I am going to play the slot machines. I have twenty-dollars that will give me the opportunity to win my fortune," I tell him.

He gives me a kiss before leaving. "Have fun, I'll be back before the show." He heads down to meet the fellows.

I dress and head down to the casino to stand in line and give my gambling money to the cashier to get change. I don't want to spend all of my money in one machine. With four fives. I decide to play the nickel machines so my money will go further.

I am sitting at the machine trying my best to get five sevens on the same line when I hear my name called. It is a female voice without an accent. This can't be good. I debate ignoring the voice or adding an accent to my own voice to throw whoever it is off my scent.

"Lynn, girl it's been years. I would know you anywhere. How have you been? What are you doing in Vegas? Are you still in Wichita? Did you know I live in Vegas now? Do you live out here or are you visiting? Imagine that." She stops long enough to take a breath.

I am immediately aware of a number of things. Whoever it is talks way too much. She also asks way too many questions. She is obviously from my past. I have not seen her in years. It is doubtful that I will ever see her again. I turn to face the inevitable. However, I don't recognize her at all. She is trying to distract me from winning my fortune in Vegas.

Ms. Chatty is an African American woman, close to fifty, with a head full of blond hair that is flowing, flapping and showing that weave can be wonderful. She is stylishly dressed in a tight low-cut dress that enhances her boob job. She also has on a pair of comfortable shoes, so she is not all crazy.

"Lynn, I knew that was you. Remember that time we cut school. We went over to Jimmy's house to get high. We had just barely left before his mother got home. That was so much fun; I haven't seen anyone from the neighborhood for years. I left right after high school. I came out west for college. I just love it. The weather is so nice. I have been here ever since."

"What's your phone number? Honey, I can't believe that I ran into you here in Vegas of all places. Would you like to go to a show tomorrow? I have some tickets because I am a manager for the guys in the group. They are amazing. It's a male revue at the Fitzgerald. Are you staying at the Rio?" she explains and asks using all of the air from the breath she just took.

I would have been convinced she is just a lunatic except I do remember cutting school. I also remember going to get high at Jimmy's house with… Oh no, it can't be!

"Hannah?" I say her name louder than I intended.

Fellow possible future jackpot winners glance in our direction. It can't be her. In Vegas. Talking to me. I have not seen her in years, definitely not since high school was out. She had left town, never to return. Who would have thought that I would actually see someone that I know. In Las Vegas. I feel like singing, 'It's a Small World After All.'

I barely get the acknowledgement out before I remember that she was always a chatterbox. Her mother used to scold her all the time because she could not keep quiet. I consider my options. Well, I wanted to go to Fitzgerald's anyway, might as well take in a show.

"Yes, I'm staying at the Rio while I'm here visiting. How much are the tickets?" I ask.

"Oh, they're free. You will love the men. It is downtown; I can come to pick you up. We can have dinner before the show. We can catch up on old times. I am so glad to see you. Here's my number. How long will you be here? Never mind. We'll talk more tomorrow. Call me. I've got to rush I'm on my way to get a massage." She scribbles her name and number on paper she pulled from her purse. She hugs me and heads down the aisle and out of sight.

Just like that, she is gone. I can hardly imagine me at a male review. It will probably be fun. I ponder what to expect for a while. Why the hell not?

I continue to put money into various machines. I don't get the winning jackpot at any of them. No lucky sevens. No stars. I decide to cut my losses. I head to the room to wait for Mr. M.O.P. to return. For some reason, I don't tell him of my plans for tomorrow. I will surprise him. We have just a short while before lobby call, so we rush to get ready for the gig.

The Vegas show seems different. That could be because it is in Vegas. Vegas is different from anywhere I have been. All aspects of the city are over the top. The show is in a large concert room that quickly fills with people. They are dressed in some of the most outlandish outfits I have seen on stage or off.

A large Goth group stands out in the crowd. They consist of a dozen or more people, men, women, and an unidentifiable mixture of the two, all with black hair and black nails. Their eyebrows, lipstick and eye makeup are exaggerated. They are dressed in unrelieved black. Everyone is wearing long leather coats. They have no emotion on their faces. I wonder why they are here. They don't seem as though they will allow themselves to enjoy anything.

Certain women here feel that less is better. They have on outfits so short, if they bend over, you can see a birth canal. I don't know if they came with their breasts or made the purchase in Vegas, but they sure do have them on display. If I win at the slots, I am buying me some just like the woman in the see-through top. They stand up without a bra or anything. It doesn't matter that they look unnatural and hard, they are big.

There must have been a special on bigger lips because this many people can't have lips that look so much alike. These are not the full, plump, natural lips. They are the lips that look as if they are swollen from repeated punches to the mouth. The plastic surgeons in this area must be billionaires.

The show is fantastic as usual. The audience does have something in common with other audiences. They are very enthusiastic in their enjoyment. They dance, sing and take an active part in the show.

When the music is over, I wait for Mr. M.O.P. in my seat. It takes me a while to get back to myself and disconnect. Once he comes out there are the hugs and handshakes. After the admiration is over, we head to the casino.

Mr. M.O.P. and I watch craps for a short time. He tries to explain the necessary skills to win at craps.

Finally, he says, "Come on. You shoot and I'll stake you."

I give it my best efforts. I guess we are winning because they kept giving us chips. Other people were losing and getting their chips taken. I throw for about seven times but I have a hard time keeping the dice on the table so my craps career is short lived.

We head to the roulette wheel. We buy some pink chips with our craps winnings. The game is much easier and I don't have to do anything strenuous or difficult like throwing dice. After two of my lucky numbers came up at the roulette wheel, I decide to get away while I am ahead.

Then we head to our room. In the midst of hugs, kisses, and spectacular touching I tell him of my plans for tomorrow.

"You're not going to believe this, but I met a woman I went to school with in the casino. She invited me to a show tomorrow. A male stripper show. What do you think of that?" I throw my chest and chin out as I finish talking.

"What do you think about that," he counters. "You may like it, you may not. I've been to strip shows. They can be a lot of fun. I like having you with me, but I am working. It must be boring for you so why not enjoy Vegas while you are here. I'm glad that you didn't ask me to go with you. Besides, I get to enjoy you when you're finished."

My attack demeanor fades and is replaced with relief I will be allowed to make my own decision.

"Well, I remember, we agreed to do something touristy in every city. I could have asked you to go with me." I tease him with the thought and get a reluctant smile. "How about we meet downtown at ten in front of Fitzgerald? Then we can grab a desert. And, I want to see the light show that I read about somewhere. They have it downtown outside. We can see it together. After that, we can get a cab back to the Rio after the light show. How does that sound?"

"Something tells me that I am going to enjoy your having been to a strip show," He tells me as he pulls me into his arms for some exceptional loving. We make love until sleep overtakes us.

***

What Happened Here?

When we get up, we make love again. He is in my arms and I am in his all morning long. Sometimes between loving, we talk. We share our secrets, what makes us happy, what makes us cry. What gives us joy and sorrow.

We also play not in the room, ignoring telephone calls on the room phone and his cell phone. We ignore knocks on the door from the persistent and the housekeeping. We stayed that way until we could not hide from the world any longer.

We get up and shower. Together. It is more of a mutual rubbing and hugging and kissing. Just using our hands and the soap, we shower. He gets ready to go to the gig and dresses in the striped polo shirt and tan slacks.

"Do you mind me going to look at half naked men with my friend?" I ask. Robert would absolutely forbid me to do anything of the sort. I don't think they have strippers in Wichita anyway.

"I think it will be fun for you. Have you ever been to a show before? You seem rather hesitant," he says. "You're a big girl, if you want to, go and enjoy. Life is to be lived. You decide. If you don't want to go there, you can always come to the gig."

I am not used to making my own decisions. Robert would have forbidden me going to such a place and then made me feel bad about even considering such a thing.

"I'm going to give it a whirl. If I don't like it, I'll just leave," I say.

"Good for you. I'm going to meet the fellows now," he tells me. He comes in for a kiss and a hug before leaving.

I get ready to go downtown and decide to wear my corset and stockings. Even though stockings are a close cousin to pantyhose, they are not evil. I feel so damn sexy in this contraption. It makes me look like the 'after breast implant' picture. You would never know I was a member of the itty-bitty titty committee the way this thing works.

I wear my cute pink sleeveless dress but decide to leave off the matching jacket since the weather is warm. Sensible pink shoes are perfect with the dress and will make walking easy.

It is easier to walk downtown because everything is close according to the hotel staff. I figure after what I have seen; my stockings will blend right in with the Vegas scene. I call Hannah once I am dressed.

"Hi Hannah. Are we still on for the show? This is Lynn. If you don't want to go, I'm okay with that." I am starting to sound like her so I shut my mouth.

"Honey, of course we're still on. I can be there in twenty minutes. I'm driving a green Jaguar. Managing naked men pays. I can't wait for you to see them. I think you'll be impressed. I'll pick you up in front of the Rio. I just love that place. It is so pretty. You picked a good hotel to stay at for you visit to Vegas. You never did tell me what you are doing in Vegas. Well anyway, I'll see you in a few. We'll eat before the show and see a bit of downtown. Bye now," she says before hanging up.

She could have hour-long conversations with herself and not notice the absence of a response.

I am feeling nervous, but it is my decision. I hang around the front of the Rio and try not to panic or look out of place. Shortly, a shiny forest green Jag with Hannah at the wheel toots a horn. As I climb in, she starts talking.

"We're going to Fremont Street, which is downtown. Downtown has a large number of casinos but they are smaller and more intimate than the Strip. The place has a covering, kind of like being in an enclosed mall. It is about six blocks. There are souvenir shops, casinos, pawnshops, drug store, and just about everything else you can think of," she shares as we dodge in and out of traffic. It takes about ten to fifteen minutes for us to get into the area. She pulls into a casino parking lot where we climb out. I stop to stare around and soak up the feel of the place. We head down the street to the covered area.

Hannah and I wander in and out of a few casinos. Mermaids Casino has women in glittering showgirl costumes complete with tall headdress. They are handing out colorful beads they use to entice you to enter. Another has a large wheel that you can spin to win prizes. She and I continue to wander in and out of casinos and I get the opportunity to increase my money. It doesn't work. I've already lost five dollars so it is time to slow down.

We go into the Fitz. They actually have a car for the grand prize on a nickel slot machine. I have to play this one. The slot machine eats my gambling money five nickels at a time. I decide to up my money by another twenty so I can gamble after the show.

I hope I am not getting addicted. I heard people don't know they have a problem until they start selling blood to get money. This is my last gambling twenty I tell myself. I will not play again tomorrow. Instead of four fives, I get twenty ones. That will slow me down. I am ready to win.

"Are you ready to eat now? We have plenty of time before the show. Anyway if you've played one slot machine, you've played them all," Hannah says. People that have interesting things to do where they live really don't see how exciting it is to those of us that don't have this much glitter and excitement.

"Sure, I haven't eaten all day long," I tell her.

We head to the restaurant at the casino. The menu has some interesting choices. I settle for the pecan-crusted salmon with asparagus. Hannah has the stuffed mushrooms and a pesto flatbread. While we eat, Hannah catches me up on the past thirty years of her life in her nonstop fashion. It was more exciting than mine was. Well, until now.

I decide not to tell her that my family thinks I'm in Europe but I'm here with a man I met on a plane. Since I can barely get a word in, it doesn't matter. After dinner, we head to the show room.

The doors open. With Hannah's connections, we don't have to stand in line to go in for the show "Size Matters." We go in and get two front row seats. She orders us each a drink and I sit back to enjoy the show.

"I'm so glad you came," she yell/whispers.

"I am too," I yell back.

The lights dim and the music begins to pulse. Four guys run out on stage in their costumes. There is a chef, a cowboy, a police officer, and a fisherman. The quartet puts a lot of energy in the dance they use to warm up the audience. Their movements are suggestive and risqué.

The cowboy is dressed in boots, spurs, and a huge hat. He says his name is Bull and he has on black chaps that emphasize his size. He is short. He reminds me of a mailbox. His body is not as much defined as it is sturdy. He has a baby face and no facial or body hair. He is blond on top and either lives in the sun or a tanning booth. His blue-fringed shirt is distracting.

There is something about a man in a fringed shirt that just does not work for me.

The chef has on a tall chef hat. He is about five feet ten and looks as though he has worked out or had some implants. I would guess he is Native American because of his high cheekbones and the sharp angles of his face. He has a long braid that lingers down his back. At the end of the braid is a white cord. Chef Long, as he calls himself, is dressed in all white with a long apron that looks like a dress. Hmmm. Something about a man in a dress with a ribbon on his flowing braid has as much appeal as a man in fringe.

The police officer is worth the price of admission. I should be trying to arrest him for a first-degree felony. It has to be illegal to be that fine. Captain Baton is six-two and has a chest that commands that you look there. He does the chest flex and makes each side of his chest go up and down. That nipple could probably lift a woman off the ground if she was sucking it.

He is grown enough to have chest and facial hair. The sprinkling of black hair over that broad chest makes me want to run my hands in it and rub my cheek against it and whatever else he would let me do to it. His thin mustache and goatee are sharply trimmed and I wonder how it would feel on my …

He reveals arms that could open a coconut or certainly a pair of legs. I especially like the handcuffs. There is something to wrap a fantasy around on a cold night. He has a perfect build. I would not mind him strip-searching me. I remember seeing police use the baton to make people open their legs. Oh, Captain, I think I did something. Take me down to the station and make me talk, is all I can think.

The final entry into the quartet of maleness is Rod, the fisherman. He is wearing this cute plaid shirt and jeans with wet boots. He has the requisite fishing hat, a tackle box and this unusually long, thick pole strategically placed. I think I now understand the name "Size Matters." He looks like a chocolate bar and I would love to have some of him. He is at least six-five and could stick his pole in my watering hole at any time.

The first two guys, Fringe and Dress, do their individual bump and grind. They are down to almost nothing, but they started out in fringes and a dress. I am not interested. I am saving my excitement for the last two.

Then it is the police officer's turn. Awesome. He moves around in ways I can't imagine. He is a feast for the erotic zones: broad chest, with a shine on all that brown skin because he is working up a sweat. The more he takes off, the hotter I get. He twirls his extra long baton in my direction. I just don't believe that it is all him.

The fisherman! He gyrates and moves as if he has no bones. On one move, he puts his hands up in the air then bends over backwards until his hands touch the floor. He effortlessly propels himself into a handstand. Damn. You can see the outline of his size and it matters.

Mr. Fisherman comes my way, swinging his pole. A spectacular, manly specimen, he moves his pole all around like a martial arts weapon. I could be a pole dancer if that were the pole. He puts his fishing pole aside and starts shaking his very tight ass my way, shedding clothing with every step.

I look, thinking, where could he put all of that; there is only so much space in a pussy? I sip (or rather gulp) the drink that had magically appeared at the table. I don't remember ordering another. I hope it is mine because I need it.

I peer to see if there is stuffing in his bottoms or if he is all of that. By this time, he is down to his g-string. It looks all human to me. In the interest of accuracy, I decide to pay for a peek.

When he comes my way again, I am waving a few bills. I pull out the side of the scrap of fabric that barely contains his balls. Where did he stuff the rest of him in there? As I lift and attempt to tuck my money into his bulge, my eyes roam to the front to see if I can see.

Needless to say, I end up putting all of my twenty-dollar gambling money in his g-string, bit by bit. I am glad I got ones. I don't win a car, but I do get to have a lot of have fun. I am turning into such a slut.

After the show, Hannah asks me if I want to meet the guys. I decline. I could not stand to have all that maleness around me. I am curious enough to ask her "Have you ever, you know, with them?"

"Individually and in groups," she tells me.

For the first time she does not elaborate. However, she does have a look on her face that makes me think I am way out of my league.

We have another drink or two in the casino. She talks the entire time. I now know her life story since the last time I saw her. She does not even know that I am here with a stranger I met on a plane. I tell her I have to go and promise to call her. It is getting close to the time to meet said stranger.

Out in the front of the casino, Mr. M.O.P. is about halfway down the casino, watching the street vendors. There is a young African American man doing paintings with cans of spray paint.

The young man, wiry and dressed in jeans and a t-shirt with a hat on, is a great showman. He runs around the paper spraying and making images. The colors are vivid. People are buying the pictures as he is making them. We watch before walking on to other booths of jewelry, rice painting, and t-shirts. A short time later, we hear sounds over the speakers outside. The light show is starting.

People fill the street. After a few flickers, the lights on the casinos go dim. The music starts and puts us in the mood. Everyone seems to catch a bit of the energy of the show. It is like watching cartoons in the sky. The show features a space theme.

The battle is between spaceships that race across the sky, from one end of the enclosure to the other. For about fifteen minutes, we are a part of the Fremont Street experience. The people are friendly, open and inviting. They are clapping and cheering. The light show leaves you impressed by the beauty and sense of connection to everyone out there. We decide to leave shortly thereafter.

We hail a cab at the corner of Fremont Street and head back to the Rio. I don't look at the view on the way back. We hold hands and kiss as the driver drives. I feel like we have done this before. I am finally bold or high enough to touch him as we ride. I feel the muscles on his thigh, his arm, his back.

When we arrive back at the Rio, we head to the restaurant to get some desert. I have a slice of carrot cake with whiskey and coffee. Mr. M.O.P. has a peach cobbler with vanilla ice cream and a dry white wine. After desert, we have another drink and some conversation. It just feels so right that we keep sitting, talking, being with each other. We need to be in our room in order to be closer.

I can tell I am tipsy when I grab Mr. M.O.P. after the hotel room door closes and back him against it. Thoughts of Nashville dance by as I kiss him. I boldly unfasten his pants and put my hand inside to touch my prize. Two balls and a stick. Jackpot, I am a winner.

Ever ready, he obligingly kicks off his shoes. He lets his pants come down then off. I become fixated again with the chains that Alita had placed on us. I just want to feel them against his skin. My hands are all over him. I feel powerful and in charge.

"Come to the bed," I command. I make quick work of his shirt. "Lay down," I slur.

I am in control and loving it. Seeing him lying there ignites something inside. I decide I have to be on top tonight. Once my dress goes over my head, I keep my corset and stockings on for the moment. Corsets are a wonderful invention. I touch my own self because my breasts look so good with the help of a corset this contraption. They get a quick squeeze from me to see them respond.

"Tonight it's my turn," I tell him.

"What do you mean? Your turn to do what," he asks with a mischievous grin.

"I am setting the pace. I'll be taking the lead."

With that, I open his legs and settle myself between his thighs. The feel of the silk stockings on my legs touching his legs intensifies the sensations that are already running riot over my body. I bend my leg so I can see my leg in the stocking. Damn, that looks good.

He gives me the smile. "Yessss."

We're off.

I have never been on a horse but I bet I could ride one. It would have to feel like this. Just the knowledge of him being under me, being in control of how deep I allow him to enter me is empowering. Having the sensation of him under me, moving up to meet me as I'm coming down to meet him makes me move faster to get the feeling again.

This is awesome, exhilarating, just plain good. I bend down on my elbows watching him as he is watching me. I lean over and kiss him. My tongue is in his mouth moving with the rhythm of our bodies joining.

Looking at his nipples, I figure what the hell. I suck first the left one, then the right one. They feel as though I am licking raisins. He completely stops moving. I reach behind him and squeeze his ass. That gets him going again.

Then I look at him and say "Yessss."

Now I knew he is limber, but what happens next causes an instant orgasm. This man puts his legs up on my shoulders without missing a stroke and still moving steadily up to meet me while I move down to meet him. How in the hell did he do that?

I lose it at that point, but I am not finished. We work each other like a full-time job. We reach the peak that awaited us. I collapse on his chest. I feel his legs come down as his arms come up and around me, holding me close as I slide into a sexually satisfied sleep. I forgot to talk into my voice recorder I think as I drift off.

The next morning he asks about my last evening show. I tell him about the men in the show. I also tell him how exciting it was to see half-naked men gyrating and getting me warm. He enters into the spirit of adventure.

Then he says, "I'm glad you went. I certainly appreciate what you saw. Is that what made you so greedy?"

"Are you complaining? Was I the only one having a good time last night?" are my questions.

"Not a bit" he assures me.

I laugh as I head off to take a shower. Afterwards I lovingly pack away my corset and stockings. It is doubtful they will ever get to be worn again, but they sure did make it happen the one time they did get on my body. Robert would not like or appreciate me having something so whorish. We make it to the lobby for our trip to the airport.

***

My Travel Tips for Las Vegas

Don't get a massage. Visit the mall. Go to the Rio, it is beautiful. Make sure you go to the Fitzgerald's and play a while. The light show downtown is a must see. Buy yourself or someone else a red corset and stockings and then have some wild sex if you can.

TRACK SIX: SAN DIEGO

San Diego is not Wichita. It has a fast pace that assaults us at the airport. Everyone seems to be in a hurry. I don't have the opportunity to get a feel for the city by being in the airport. The airport is not large in comparison to the other airports that we have been in over the past few days. It is easily as busy as the others are but it feels different.

People don't seem friendly; they don't smile or give greetings I received in other cities. Instead, they walk into or past you without any indication that they see you. It is a little intimidating to be invisible when so many people are around.

We gather our things from baggage claim and wait for Marty. Marty secures our local transportation and herds us outside. We climb into a large white van. He drives twenty minutes and we get to the hotel.

Looking at the hotel, the word seedy comes to mind, as do fleabag, scary, and damn. The bellman has tattoos that cover his forearms. He has a long gray ponytail with multiple color ponytail holders going down the hair every few inches.

Surprisingly, he is friendly. He smiles and chats just like a normal person. His tattoos are what gave me a fright. I have to remember not judge people by the first impression. After some conversation, he gives us the keys to our room.

The room is just that. A room with a bed and couch. There is no mirror on the closet door. There is not a mini kitchen. A chair would be a blessing, a clean tub a luxury. The small couch in the middle of the wall at least looks clean. Marty must have stock in this place. The bed makes you sorry you did not bring your own sheets, mattress, pillows and bed. I know we will not be spending much time in the room. I am glad.

I go to the front desk to explore and see what I can find of interest to see in the city. The desk clerk continues to be friendly and is knowledgeable about the San Diego. He shares information about the world's largest flea market. It is at the stadium parking lot. We can get there with a fifteen-minute bus ride from the hotel. It is supposed to have everything a person can think they might ever want or need. I find out how to catch a bus to the stadium and back.

Mr. Tattoo Ponytail also shares that we can go to Tijuana by catching the train and bus. We could make a day trip if we start early. There is shopping to be done on Revolution Boulevard and quite a few people go down to Tijuana just for the shopping.

I get other pertinent information and thank him for his help. People in San Diego ain't so bad after all.

***

Flea Market Heaven

I go back to the room and share my newly found site-seeing information with Mr. M.O.P. He smiles at my enthusiasm and agrees that my tourist activities sound interesting. We decide to grab coffee and a roll to keep hunger at bay and then sally forth for our adventure. Our

San Diego tourist attraction is waiting. No one else is interested so it is just the two of us.

We go out and catch the bus in the front of the hotel. The bus lets us off across the street from the stadium. We are feeling daring, so we cross in the middle of the street to get to the flea market.

It costs us one dollar each to enter. He gives up the two bucks and we're allowed into the hallowed parking lot of vendors selling and people browsing. This is flea market heaven. There is stuff everywhere. Each individual stall, about ten feet by ten feet in size, has the unique signature of the owner.

At one stall, they are selling fresh fruit. The young woman is screeching/singing, "Peaches get your fresh peaches here." The peaches are an attention getter, not because of their size, but because she has a voice that should not be allowed to sing. At all. Anywhere. She would not be able to find a key at a locksmith shop.

Her singing does the trick for a sale. I stop just because I want to make sure that the voice is human and not the result of animal cruelty. "How much for the peaches," I ask just to see if this form would speak as a human or revert to its true animal self. "Four for a dollar," is the response, in English.

Hmm. It looks like a human, speaks like a human, but the singing makes me want to take my ears off and bash them with a large rock. I give up a buck to get the biggest peaches I have ever seen and to keep this woman/beast from assaulting my ears with further entreaties.

Finding Passion: Confessions of a Fifty Year Old Runaway

The peaches are the juiciest and sweetest I have ever
had. The juice is running down my hand and arm. Mr.
M.O.P. stops me to lick the juice off my hand and each
finger. That feels good. Maybe we should go back to the
hotel for this lick session. Instead, we continue
familiarizing ourselves with the flea market.

Another stall has souvenirs, flags, hats, and t-shirts.
There is nothing that interests me. A few stalls down, you
can have pictures taken dressed in old western attire,
complete with the six shooters for the man. This is too good
to pass up. We have to get our pictures taken.

"You get yours taken," I tell him.

"Only if we take one together," he says.

I should not or they'll be too many memories. If
someone discovers them, pictures would be hard to explain.
It says quite a bit about my marriage that Robert couldn't
tell if I took them twenty minutes or twenty years ago. Alita
already knows. What the hell?

"Okay," is my capitulation and we go inside.

We go rooting through the racks to find the perfect
outfit to become immortalized wearing. I find something I
think is special. We turn to each other at the same time. He
has a cowboy hat, jeans, six-shooter with a plaid red and
white shirt.

I am holding a red dance hall girl dress. I can't help but
to speculate on what this means. Maybe we did know each
other before. We certainly seem to mesh now. The
photographer poses us in a variety of settings before we

take the picture with me sitting on his lap. It is so touristy we both have to laugh over it when we see the results.

"Are you hungry?" he asks.

"Baby, I'm carrying these hips because I respond to sweets, meats, and all things chocolate," I say with a hand on a full figured hip.

The sun is sending heat rays down that are only relieved as we enter another stall to search the wares. We eat our way around the flea market. This includes pretzels with salt and mustard, Queen Anne cherries, and fresh roasted pistachios. I happen to find a very large piece of obsidian, which is the only non-edible thing that catches my eye.

We leave to get back for the six o'clock lobby call and run across the street hand in hand to get to the bus stop. The bus comes shortly after we get there.. As we ride, there are a series of touches and smiles. And some kisses. And some more touches. He is giving me everything I miss at ho--. I put a stop to this thought. I forgot one of the rules. There can be no comparisons.

Our conversation is non-verbal. "I feel you," I think.

"I want you to be with me."

"Where are we heading?"

"Will you go with me?"

"I don't know where we are going, I'm afraid."

Finding Passion: Confessions of a Fifty Year Old Runaway

"Trust."

This is too intense a conversation to conduct verbally. It is already becoming more than just a two-week affair. I think that it would be easy to forget an affair. I don't know what the hell this is. I just know I feel it so deeply inside of myself I may have trouble letting go.

I am glad to see the hotel in the near distance. I pull the cord to request the stop. I stand up to create a further break in our connection. We get off the bus and get our waist and ass thing going for the walk across the street.

Once back at the hotel, we dress for the show. I wear my ill-fated dress from New York since I have not been clothes shopping. I am going sans panty hose. Those are an unnecessary evil. He is very suave in an Africentric shirt of mustard color with black design. Black slacks accentuate the color in the shirt. We are ready for the ride to the gig.

In the lobby, the fellows are teasing us. They tell me that since I have been here, they don't even see him except at practice times. There is speculation on what we are doing all the time. I remind them that I have invited them on our adventures, but they have not decided to join us on our travels. He joins in the teasing and it feels like family. Marty gets the van and we all pile in for the ride to the set. The teasing continues during the ride.

As we enter the theater, he and the fellows head to the owner's area. I head to get a good seat. A short time later, people start to enter. It quickly becomes crowded but there is great audience connection. As always, the music is smooth, soothing, and touching. It reminds me at turns of sunshine, summer, and energy or great sadness, pain, and helplessness.

When I hear the songs, it's more than just hearing the words. I don't understand most of them. I feel the emotion. On some of the sets, I don't think of summer, I feel it. The sun on my skin, the brightness of its rays, the newness and heat of the day, the promise of life worth living. The sorrowful songs give me the opportunity to interpret them to my life.

I have been meaning to ask him what the songs are about, but I never remember. I think I like putting my own interpretation to them anyway. If I knew what it was about, that would limit what I should feel. Not knowing gives me the freedom to make it what I want it to be for me individually.

The crowd shows the emotion unleashed by the music. The words are foreign but the music crosses cultures. The joy, the excitement, every nuance is captured and reflected by the multicultural audience. Caucasians, Hispanics, African Americans, and me. I don't want to be this caught up in the music, the times, the him. I think it is already too late and has been since we saw each other on the plane.

Afterwards, I wait in the theater lobby for him to come from backstage. As always, there are well-wishers that interact and encourage. Marty does his usual split of the herd to get us outside and to the van. The ride back is full of the celebratory excitement that I am becoming familiar with after a set. I almost feel their contentment and excitement. After all, I was actually in the audience feeling Mr. M.O.P.

Finding Passion: Confessions of a Fifty Year Old Runaway

At the hotel, everyone exchanges goodnights. Willie and Leon greet a couple of women coming in the door. It looks like all will have a good night.

In the room, we embrace. It is not a prelude. The embrace is the completion, and it feels right. I get into the shower first. The water washes away the sweat that being in a crowd creates. I take my time, thinking how much I am enjoying my time with him. I get out of the shower and into my sexy nightie.

He gets into the shower next. While he is there, I try to catch-up on my voice recordings before they become a hazy memory. I am talking about the flea market time and the ride back when he gets out of the shower.

He climbs into bed. Instead of going to sleep, he is watching me. "What are you doing?" he asks me.

"I am trying to keep this time alive after it's over. I keep a record of the activities each day if I can remember. The past few days have been busy. I have not been writing or recording, so now I have to catch up."

"What will you do with it?" he asks.

"Listen to it when I'm older and grayer," is how I answer him. Satisfied with my attempts, I stop my recorder. I climb into bed beside him.

"Why not write about it? You want to write, why not write about what you have seen?"

"Maybe one day I will," I tell him.

We turn to each other and embrace safe, happy in each other's arms. Then we love. Easy, unhurried. Confident of getting there.

***

Going South

The next day we get up early and dress so we can head to Tijuana for our day trip. We decide not to have breakfast at the hotel. The coffee and rolls from yesterday are still heavy on my stomach. We decide to get something along the way. We go out of the hotel to catch our bus.

Mr. Friendly the desk clerk had told us that there are places at the train station that we can eat. The bus, which is full of commuting San Diegoans, takes us to the train station in about twenty minutes. We grab some coffee and a bagel before we get on the train. A short hour-long train ride gets us to our destination, Tijuana. We both have our passports so re-entry will not be a problem. The train lets us off at the border. Entry into Mexico is not an issue. No one even asks to see our identification. Mexico must not have problems with terrorists or illegal aliens.

We catch a taxi to Revolution Boulevard, which has shops up and down each side of the street. Every other shop has gold or silver that the merchants are willing to put on a cigarette lighter and allow the flame to show that their merchandise is the real thing. Anything you could possibly want you can buy on this street for the right price.

I find a shot glass that says 'fill me with Tequila then feel me'. I also find a genuine mother of pearl chess set that is unusual. I get it even though I don't play chess. For only ten dollars, it is a steal. I see a cigarette case that the salesman assures me is genuine gold. "See it doesn't burn when I put the flame on it" the salesman tempts me. I buy it.

Mr. M.O.P. holds up a lime green t-shirt that says 'Mexico, don't you want to go' and asks me "Don't you think this would be good for my daughter?"

"You can't ask me that." Did anyone explain the rules? "I can't pick out a shirt for your daughter. That would be sacrilegious. I think."

"I want your opinion. You've met Alita, so what's the problem?"

"I don't really know." Since I have parented girls, I give my assistance. I also buy some t-shirts for my daughters. I wonder what they would say if they knew that I also picked out twin t-shirts for the daughter of someone else.

He finds a Mexican drum that must be souvenir hawkers' bread and butter. I would not be surprised if the cover is cat skin. He tells me he needs it because of a certain sound that only this particular instrument can make. That does not make a rat's ass worth of sense to me, but I am not a musician.

After shopping, it is time to eat. We find a restaurant that we can sit in while we eat. It is semi crowded and people are drinking marguerites like water. There are pictures of celebrities on the walls, some signed, others not. There is an upstairs area where a band is playing. They don't sound as good as the music I have been hearing from him and the fellows. We go downstairs.

We get a seat along the wall near the windows. There are children selling gum outside of the window. I make a purchase from a girl that looks too small to be selling anything. Immediately, ten more children are enticing me to buy from them. I remain strong and don't succumb or I would have a ton of gum to lug around.

We both have tacos. They arrive within twenty minutes. I did not know when we ordered that we have to assemble the food ourselves. Lettuce, guacamole, rice, sour cream, cheese, beans, beef and we get to put it all together. I guess I look lost and he puts mine together as well as his. He's certainly agile. This sure isn't Taco Bell, but it's delicious. I am glad we made the trip.

He finishes before I do. "I forgot to get something. I need to run back down the street. Will you be comfortable sitting here till I get back?" he asks me showing so much concern I wanted to kiss him.

"Sure, I'll just give my feet a rest while you're gone." I figure there is something he wants to get for Alita. The funny thing is I don't mind. I am grateful for her sharing nature. I got a gift for her and I didn't get anything for Robert.

I am people watching and see some faces in the passersby that look familiar. He looks just like Brian at my job only shorter. She looks like my aunt only lighter. I guess we all do have twins and triplets in the world. There goes Isaiah walking down the other side of the street.

When he gets back from his detour, it is time for us to get a taxi to the border. Three hours in Tijuana have passed by quickly. At the border, we sail past customs without incident. I guess because we look neither Mexican, nor terroristy.

Back in the U.S. of A., we make it to the train station to go back to San Diego. During the train ride, I fall asleep with my head on his shoulder. He wakes me up to get off the train before I sleep through our stop. We cross the street to the bus stop. A short ride later, we are back to the hotel. We walk into the lobby arm on waist, me; and hand on ass, him.

In the room, I shower first. I really need to calm down because I am having hot flashes. Maybe I am starting menopause; I didn't know that it would make me so horny. The shower really doesn't help at all. I think of another shower, which also does not help at all. I slip into my sexy nightie and take a seat on the couch. We have two more hours before lobby call. As he gets out of the shower, I am ready to pounce. He is naked as usual.

"Can I do your hair?" I innocently ask from my position on the couch. I really want the opportunity to be close to him again.

He replies, "Yessss." He gets his bottle of whatever he puts in his hair. He also gets a towel that I notice rides low on his waist. I guess so his ass would not be on the floor.

He sits between my legs after he gives me the bottle. I squeeze some of the white cream between my hands and then put it into his hair. I start rubbing and his eyes close. I take the opportunity and gently open the towel with my feet, causing his eyes to open. I see the chains still in place. He smiles as he closes his eyes again while I work his hair the same way I had watched him work it. My eyes take in the sights, which include a penis that has no erectile dysfunction. Growing.

My feet get in his lap. His hands may have put them there. I think it was my trampy feet though. Maybe my feet like are explorers searching for new adventures or a way to cure world hunger? Maybe not, but they are in his lap. And they are happy. My feet are such sluts.

Judging by the looks of it, they are not the only things happy. My feet capture his member between the two of them and start to stroke. He looks like a smoked sausage sticking out of the bun my feet make. He gives new meaning to the term foot long.

With my hands, I keep rubbing cream in his hair. With my feet, I keep rubbing his penis. I feel the chain that is still in place. His eyes remain closed. Hell, mine start to close I am feeling so good. This rubbing and stroking action is lulling me to sleep.

He turns his body suddenly. My eyes pop open. My short sexy nightie is not an impediment to him. A quick efficient tug on my legs has his mouth at the inside juncture of my thighs. He must play the harmonica in his spare time. He is humming on my stuff.

A buzzing in my head reminds me that I have not taken a breath. I suck air into my mouth as he sucks my flesh into his. He told me he ate everything. He did not tell me he likes to play with his food. He squeezes it with his hands, strokes it with his tongue, and nibbles it with his teeth. He has mastered this art also.

He should have a television food show. With pussy as a main course. Shit, he should give lessons. I know what I like now that he shown me. I heard when I was young that you will go blind if you masturbate, but if you could lick yourself, what would happen? Maybe you would lose your sense of smell. I'm willing to risk it. I wonder if yoga could get me limber enough to do this to my own damn self. I am going to find a yoga class as soon as I get home. If I could get it right, I would never leave my room.

Somehow, we both end up on the couch. He covers me with his body. With starts and stops, he teases me before entering. He pushes into me, parking his man meat as if it were an Escalade in a single car garage. It is a snug fit. He stays still in me as if he lives there before starting to stroke in firm slow movements. He goes all of the way out before coming back in to hold me captive.

As he kisses me, I smell my scent and taste myself on him. I lick his lips and suck first the top one and then the bottom one. He bends his head down to take ownership of a nipple. First the left one then the right one. We end in a kiss.

Between us, his hand goes down to capture the sensitive flesh where we join. I contract around him and release sensual fluids that have been straining to be released. A powerful thrust and his fluids mix with mine. When we finish, I need another shower. He also needs another shower. Done right, sex can work up a sweat.

We shower together, slowly. It is more standing in the water and holding each other than it is washing. We get out to dry each other off. I sit on the bed.

"It's time to get ready for the lobby call," he reminds me.

"I think I'll sit this one out. I need some sleep," I tell him.

"Oh, I'll miss you. I'm going to go and get ready," he informs me. No recriminations, no petty pouting. Just more of that damn understanding I am beginning to associate with him. He gets dressed in brown slacks and a cream top. He gives me a kiss, a nipple squeeze, and then leaves.

I don't go to sleep when he leaves. I sit, think, and try not to think of what I am feeling. I think about how important home is to me. I think about how much my family needs me. Eventually, I must have gone to sleep. I don't hear him come in. Sometime during the night, I feel his arms around me and I go deeper into sleep.

The next morning we examine our Mexican treasures. I come across the gift I had purchased for his wife. "This is for Alita," I extend to him the cigarette case that is "genuine gold."

"Why?" he questions.

"It reminds me of her, so elegant. Besides, I want to give her something. She is an exceptional person. I guess it's not really proper etiquette, but what the hell," I say as I move away.

"You really don't have to," he pulls me closer.

"I know but I just want her to know that I appreciate and respect her so please just take it." I turn away.

"Thank you on her behalf." He turns me back around for a kiss. Then he surprises me with "I have something for you. He steps behind me to encircle my neck with a heart locket on a thin gold chain.

More gold chains. I don't know how I feel about this gift. It settles on my chest. The knowledge that it is from him sends a slow feel-good burn through me. "Why?" I ask in an echo of his earlier question.

"I don't know. It just seems right," is his answer.

"I don't think this is a good idea." I am thinking I don't need more memories.

"Think of it as a memento of our time together," he smiles.

"We need to get ready so we can make lobby call." I don't want to think too hard on the ending that is fast approaching.

***

My Travel Tips for San Diego

Go to the flea market at the stadium. You are sure to find something interesting with all of the goods out there. If you have the opportunity to go south, do so. Go early and go often.

TRACK SEVEN: PHOENIX

We arrive in Phoenix about eleven in the morning. This is our last official stop. The last gig I will see them play. The last city I will experience with him. I am tuckered out by the fast pace of it all. I don't like living out of a suitcase. I would kill for some homemade food. I should be glad this is our last stop.

Marty gathers us after we have our luggage. He gets the van and we pile in for the ride to the hotel. Now reality seeps into my spirit. It is almost over. All of the things I have tried to avoid thinking about are rushing to the forefront of my consciousness. These include:

1) I need to get my head on straight. I don't want this to be over yet. I would like maybe three or four more days. Then I'll be ready to tell him goodbye.

2) I don't want to go home. Home does not hold the appeal it once did. Security seems routine.

3) I have seen some of the world. I know how they make whiskey. I've gambled and watched strippers in a casino in Las Vegas. I have had the most passionate physical, mental, and spiritual interlude of my life.

4) I can fly on an airplane without fear, without thought and without seeing double on takeoff.

5) I have been having unprotected sex with a stranger. Maybe I should schedule an appointment with my gynecologist as soon as I get home. I may have contracted AIDS or even genital herpes or warts.

6) I have has a hell of a good time.

We get into the hotel and into our room. I go back down to the lobby to try to get some thinking room and to find our tourist attraction for Phoenix. There are brochures that keep me looking and keep thinking at bay. The ones for the Grand Canyon and Sedona stand out to me. I choose the Grand Canyon. Sedona is only rocks.

I tell him our tourist itinerary for the day. Nothing. Tomorrow we will tour the Grand Canyon. I call the tourist company to get the reservations. Our tour guide will pick us up tomorrow morning at seven. There is a lack in enthusiasm compared to our other adventures.

The bed looks inviting. We undress and climb in to get some rest before he gets with the fellows. He falls asleep first. I am content to watch him. I can't quite identify what it is I find so fascinating about him. Mr. M.O.P. seems alive, ready to have new experiences. He is open to change and trying something different just for the thrill of it. His energy is somehow contagious. I am beginning to accept and embrace his attitude.

When I get home, I am going to do something spontaneous and exciting. Maybe I will take lessons in martial arts. I wonder what everyone will say. Robert will think I have lost my mind. Maybe I should just stick with the yoga.

Since I am doing a little introspection, I examine what I love most about my marriage. I always thought it was the fidelity, the belonging to each other exclusively. Now it seems that belonging too much to each other means not belonging to you.

CHRISTY CUMBERLANDER WALKER

These past two weeks have shown me that I not only have a great capacity to give love, I have a great desire to have love returned. If Robert ever meets someone that could make him feel like I have these past two weeks, I would understand. I would want him to live it to the fullest.

It is the small things like having your hand on someone's waist or having someone's hand on your ass, walking together, and sharing ideas. These are the things that are invaluable. Maybe Robert and I lost our way and need to refocus on each other.

Frankly, I think Robert lost his way. He has always been my focus. My life. It is all that I've got. Yeah. I need to get my head on straight. I have a home to go back to in a few days. On that thought, I get some sleep.

He wakes me with a kiss on the leg. Being orally stimulated, I am instantly awake. He spreads my legs so he can sit cross-legged between them and look. My hair is starting to grow back. It feels itchy, even more so with him watching as it grows.

"Is there something down there interesting to you?" I ask. It is hard to be nonchalant when you are spread eagle on a bed with the sexiest man alive between your legs, watching you as your pubic hair grows.

"As a matter of fact there is. I am wondering if it is physically possible to suck a person dry. What do you think?" he answers.

Whorishly (if that ain't a word, it ought to be) ready and wet for just such an attempt, I reply, "We could try it on each other. See if it works."

I have not been on the topside of a sixty-nine since I was nineteen. I think it is like riding a bicycle, something that you don't forget. Once you get on, it all comes back to you.

He lies on his back and says, "Come to me, come for me."

I position myself over him and allow him access to my secret place as I take him into my mouth. I love the feel of his skin on my tongue. I feel the chain on him that Alita had put there and take him deeper into my throat.

I pause to say around the tip of him, "It just isn't supposed to be like this, so crucial, so critical."

"This is how it's supposed to be. That is the beauty of it. We can do whatever. We can go to the moon." He draws me into his mouth and sucks firmly.

Has Mr. M.O.P. been listening to John Legend? I remember those words from a song of his. Now I know exactly what John was talking about, exactly what the feeling is in the song. This is not possible. Something is going to go wrong inserts my naturally occurring paranoia. My sexually satisfied self tells my naturally occurring paranoia to shut the fuck up because we're heading to the moon.

I am now on my back with him over me entering me in one smooth movement. He does not give my body time to adjust, but takes me to the stars and beyond. Holding me. Kissing me. Completing me. We have done this before. After loving, we sleep. If you do loving right, you have to take a nap afterwards.

When I awake, he is watching me. No conversation, just watching. We smile at each other. A glance at the clock shows it is time to prepare for the gig. We have to grab a quick shower together if we plan on being ready on time.

I decide to wear a pair of slacks with low heels. It is best to avoid pantyhose even though I am older and much wiser now. Besides, it is warm out and I don't need them with slacks. My top is the peek-a-boo number that gives the impression of cleavage. He chooses to wear a white dashiki with gray slacks. His loafers still look freshly shined. I wonder what he uses on them.

We make it to the lobby with only two minutes to spare. If we had started talking, we would have been late. We greet the fellows before seeing Marty pull the van up in front of the hotel.

The venue is a dinner theater in the downtown area, a short ride from the hotel. It is an intimate space, perfect for their performance and for my mood. Everyone seems a bit subdued. Maybe it is just the windup of their tour. We are to eat before the performance and we all order. Everyone picks at their food before it is time for sound checks. He and the fellows get up to leave. I give him a kiss and go to find where I want to sit since it is to be open seating.

I am in the audience when the show starts, storing up more memories. I feel his eyes on me and realize that they always seem to find me no matter where I have sat. He seeks me out before he goes into his passion, away from the world. There is the moment when I know he sees me and we connect. Maybe I am just being fanciful because it is the last time I will see him play.

In that same vein, the songs tonight seem more intense. The sorrow seems closer to the surface of my body. Even the happy songs make me sad. They are playing as energetically as ever. The crowd is as connected as ever, so it must just be my mood.

I am still in my seat as they do the after show interactions. Marty gets us all to the van for the trip to the hotel. On the ride, back I am quiet, being in a reflective space. He respects my mood. He takes my hand in his and just holds on. At the hotel, we go to the room and go to bed in the same quietness.

***

How Grand Is the Canyon

The next morning we are now both in a reflective space. Maybe it is a carryover from last night. In any event, we are not talking much to each other beyond the normal morning greeting. We dress in silence. Since we will be out of doors, we both put on casual and comfortable clothes. We need to be able to move freely.

We head to the lobby and are ready for the bus ride to our tourist adventure at the appointed time. The bus comes to pick us up and we board in that same silence. The ride out to the Grand Canyon is bittersweet. This is the winding down of our time together, a wrap up of my great adventure with him.

"What are you thinking?" He senses my mood as usual, possibly because he shares it.

"I am thinking of the next few days. The ending of our time together," I tell the window to keep from facing him.

"What are your thoughts?" he intrudes as he turns my face to him.

"I feel like I've been eating the last little bit of the butter pecan ice cream or polishing off the last of the chocolate cake before company can ask for another slice and wanting to be sorry because I'm supposed to be sorry. Greed and gluttony are deadly sins. But I am so glad that I was greedy and so glad that I was a glutton, and I should feel some remorse now that it is over." I try to explain so we will both understand what I feel.

"It doesn't have to be over. Why can't we do this again the next time I come to the States?" he asks.

"No, it really has to end. Soon. I don't enjoy this enough to face the inevitable disenchantment on your part or mine. The time when telephone calls go unanswered, when messages are not returned. "When someone, probably me, will end up wondering how I could have made it right or better or last longer.

This is so perfect I want it to stop now. It is as if I am walking away from a winning roulette or craps game. You know eventually that your number will not be a winner. Eventually you will throw craps. Sooner or later, you lose. But if we stop now, we both win."

I try to help him see. Being in Vegas has me thinking that I am some sort of an expert on gambling. It is such an apt analogy and the best I can think of considering my agitated state of mind.

"Why are you so negative, such a pessimist?" he asks. There is a hint of confusion in his voice and on his face.

"I'm not a pessimist. I just don't believe people can maintain this level of contentment. No one operates on this plateau. Therefore, because I am an optimistic pessimist or paranoid optimist, I would rather stop now. Leave with the good memories instead of trying to do it again and regretting how it ends." I tell him this and hope the conversation ends.

"It doesn't have to end," he entices.

"Yes it does. I am a damn near fifty-year-old African American woman. I don't share my toothbrush and I sure as hell don't want to share a man. Besides, I've got a man and it is not you. I am needy enough to want someone to depend on, someone who will be there. If nothing else, he will be there physically. That is not you."

My heart is beating faster and harder as I attempt to keep from screaming. I try biting the inside of my cheek to give me another source of pain to focus on. My voice has gotten harsh, much more quiet, and much more intense.

I wish he could understand. We spend the rest of the trip in silence. I am wondering why he can't see the obvious. I continue to look out the window so I don't have to look at or talk to him. He tries to touch my arm and talk, but I ignore him.

When the bus gets to the Grand Canyon, we get out. The driver directs us where to look. Mr. M.O.P. turns and tries to get ready and prepared to experience the beauty of this wonder.

"Look at that," he says.

I turn to see him pointing. I observe what he does. The Grand Canyon in all of its' glory. To me, the Grand Canyon is a big hole. In the ground. Hmmm. It is the Grand Canyon. I think it is one of the wonders of the world. Calling the Grand Canyon a big hole in the ground does not do it justice.

I revise my initial impression. It is a big ass hole. In the ground. I wish we had stayed in Phoenix. It definitely is not worth the ride out here to see a fucking hole, correction, fucking big ass hole. In the ground.

Maybe it is worth the trip if you can focus on the sights and not think about one of the most exciting times of your life ending. And when it ends, you know you are going back to a fucking boring ass city in a fucking boring ass state.

Once there you get to go back to your fucking boring ass job and selfish ass family who don't really give a shit about you unless you are doing what it is they want you to do. And you, bitch ass, compromising, you, will never have the opportunity to do anything you want to do, or think you might want to do, ever again in your whole fucking boring ass life. If that is not where your head is at, then the Grand Canyon might be impressive.

My ruminations may have shown on my face. "Let's just agree to disagree. Come, let's enjoy what remains of our time together," he holds out as an olive branch and an interruption to my thoughts. I grab it to hoist myself from the dark place where my thoughts were taking me. We look at the Grand Canyon together.

We take pictures at the rim. I am once again ignoring the cheaters rulebook. No pictures equal no evidence. Who cares? I only have another day with him if I decide to go back home and never see him again. I need the memories. We snap away and find willing tourists to take our picture together.

All too soon, it is time to leave the Grand Canyon. We climb aboard the bus to head back. As we ride back to Phoenix, we try to talk again. "No more thoughts of tomorrow," I proffer to extend the peace invitation.

"No thoughts of tomorrow," he agrees. We shake on it and enjoy the truly spectacular view on the way back that we had missed on the way there.

At the hotel, I find out the fellows have a ritual of everyone getting together to enjoy the last day with a meal. Everyone is jovial except the two of us. We are a part of the conversation but it does not flow freely for either one of us. It seems to be forced.

Marty was actually kind. I thank everyone for their acceptance of me. We laugh about the incident in New York. Leon causes a brief silence when he mentions seeing me when they come back later in the year. At first, I am speechless. Why does he think I will ever see them again? I recover enough to make a vague response.

After dinner, we head back to our room. Our final night in the room includes a shower scene with me crying so the water can wash away my tears. I knew tears were about to bubble over. That is why I turned down his offer of a joint shower session. The cry seems to get out enough moisture for me to face him again, dry-eyed.

Neither of us feels much like talking. Our final mating occurs in the middle of the night, in total darkness. It is completely silent, a real quiet riot. Words are not necessary. We are lying spooned together, half asleep. He enters me from that position. The tears come again. Silently. He puts his hands to my face to catch them. Through the tears comes the orgasm, spiritually, mentally, and physically. Then we sleep.

After what seems like a few minutes, it is time to get ready for our flight. We get up and go through our morning routines. We dress trying to make small talk and act as though we are both okay with this. We try to act as though it is just another day and don't talk about the fact that it will be our last day together. We act as though we are not parting today.

With forced bonhomie, we go to the lobby to get the ride to the airport. We talk with everyone. I don't know what the conversation is about that is going on around me. We get on the plane without incident. I see the fellows sharing knowing looks and acknowledge we are really bad actors.

***

My Travel Tips for Phoenix

Go see the Grand Canyon. It is worth the trip. Moreover, if you can go to the moon, go.

TRACK EIGHT NEW YORK

When we arrive in New York, we are both abnormally quiet. My flight will be leaving at three in afternoon, in eight hours. Thankfully, it is a non-stop flight. It will only take five hours. I will spend the time until my flight with him. No more lobby calls, no more venues. It will be just him and me until one o'clock when I come back to the airport to go home.

We walk slowly hand in hand to get our luggage. At the baggage claim, the fellows are gathering their things and saying their farewells to each other. They have friends to meet over the next few days and will then go to their respective countries. They will get together again later in the year and discuss plans for the next tour. Amid hugs all around, we get our bags and head out to catch a cab for a quiet ride to our destination.

***

The Worm in the Big Apple

Back at the same hotel where this adventure began, he starts the questions "Was it worth it?"

I am lying on the couch with my head in his lap. I don't even try to act as though I don't understand. There is no time for games between us. I tell him.

"I can't think about that right now."

"Why?"

He is looking directly at me with those eyes that see way too deeply inside of me. His hand is in my hair, twisting the chain there, twisting my heart.

"Because it's over. I am trying to wrap my head around that," I try to break the eye contact. I can't. I need to see him and have him see me, feel me, know me.

"It doesn't have to be over. I'm here three maybe four times a year."

"No, I don't want that. I have to go back to my home, my job, my life. This was just a fantasy that can never happen again." I succeed in turning away from his face, his spell. I get up and start pacing around the room.

"Why?" I hear as he comes to follow my movement around the room.

"I'm not willing to jeopardize what I have for whatever this is three maybe four times a year. I want the security I have in my life. I can't say why I did this. I know that I have no regrets about it. Given the chance to have a life do-over, I would do it again. It has been magical.

But, it has to be over or I would want more than I can have. With you. I am greedy and selfish enough to want more. That's not possible. At home I have someone to grow old with, someone who will keep me from being alone."

I bite this out to him over a throat clogged with so much emotion I am surprised any words can get past. The words come out harsh, as they should. How dare he tempt me with the impossible?

"Will it keep you living, tasting life, will you find passion?" he wants to know. I feel the yearning, the desire to understand in his questioning.

"Everything is relative," is my stoic response. I cease moving unable to move from the one who is my soul or my addiction.

He persists, "Is that enough for you?"

"What difference does it make? It's more enough than anything we could have. It's all I really have, so I have to make it work for me," is my conversation ender. We just stand and hold each other for a while.

"Please remove the chains," I implore him.

I can't very well go back home with them still on even though they feel a part of me now. I know there are other chains, invisible ones that only I can remove. The chains of the music. The chains of the cities. The chains of the us.

He nods and takes me into the bathroom to undress me. He starts with the physical, beginning to speak again for the first time after so many minutes of spoken silence.

"The physical is quickly forgotten. Others will take the place of me to arouse your physical longing and appease your body." He removes the chain from between my legs and places it in my hand. It feels light.

"The mental connection will dull over time. It will become a distant memory. Triggers may recall conversations we have had. Hearing of the places we have been may recall glimpses and visuals of this time. Thoughts of us being in those places together will gradually pass." He removes the chain that connects the one at my head to the one at my waist.

"You do know that it will never be completely over," he states.

I don't respond.

He puts the chain in my hand. I am amazed that they are so weightless.

He continues, "Our connection, it has and will be." He takes the chain from around my head, placing it in my hand. "Spiritually, we will remain connected, as we have over time. Even though I am removing this symbol from your waist, we will stay connected. We will be together again, in this life or another. And we will recognize each other then just as we did on the plane this time." His hands are at the chain around my waist.

I don't know why, but I stop him from removing our last connection. "Please leave it on. I'm not ready to end to have it removed. May I remove yours?" I ask.

"Only the physical. Spiritually, mentally, we will still be connected," he tells me.

I lower his pants so I can unfasten the chain and give it to him. Wordlessly. Then we walk back into the bedroom. We lay down on the bed, holding each other. I must have gone to sleep. When I wake up, he is watching me. Quiet, still, holding me.

"It's time," he whispers.

He comes with me to the airport, even though I don't want him to. "I need to see this through," he tells me.

The taxi ride is quiet. By now, I am in tears. I don't want to think too hard on the reason that I am crying. He walks me into the airport and helps me get my baggage checked. I still have a little time so we walk, again my hand on his waist, and his hand on my ass.

"Do you know that your hand finds its way to my ass instead of staying around my waist?" I ask him.

"I never meant for it to be on your waist," he says with a smile.

This will be the last time. I know that I have to go. Now. I break our hold and head to the security gate.

"Will you leave without saying goodbye, without one last kiss?" he whispers.

I turn and walk into arms that are as familiar to me as my face. He takes my face between his hands. He presses his lips on my forehead, nose and mouth. With his hands, he strokes my head, circles my waist and let his hands go for their southerly slide.

I smile. "Goodbye," I tell him then head to the security area. I don't hear him respond. I don't look back. I could not have seen him through the tears.

I must have made it through everything. My next memory is of the takeoff. The guy next to me very kindly keeps his damn mouth shut the entire flight. I am willing my mind to numbness. I don't want to feel anymore for a while. Nevertheless, my mind is on overdrive. I don't know if I am leaving captivity or freedom. His aura holds me captive and sets me free to do whatever. Now I am going home.

What did I expect? Nothing. The problem with expectations is the reality that you are forever doomed to disappointment. If there are no expectations, you can fully enjoy what is, knowing that it just is what it is. Problems arise when you want more. More love, more time, or more attention.

When you want someone to live up to or down to your expectations. People can't live up to what you want them to be anymore than you can live up to what they want you to be. Ergo, the key, I tell myself, is to expect nothing. You will never be disappointed. In my life, I expect nothing. However, serendipity came to me in the form of a percussionist on a plane. Now it is back to reality.

So why did I do it? Perhaps because I knew it was temporal. Perhaps because the connection between us was so intense. Maybe I did it because he was so captivating.

I look back on my life with Robert. I can see it was easy to be faithful before now. I had never been truly tempted. How casually I dismissed friends and acquaintances who had strayed from commitments of marriage as being weak. In many ways, I felt superior because I had not broken MY vows. But I had never wanted to break my vows before.

With Mr. M.O.P., I wanted it to be whatever. I wish I could regret these past two weeks or feel some remorse. However, I don't feel remorse. I feel sadness and pain that it is ending. Not because I hate my husband or my life, just because these two weeks have been totally and completely selfish.

This time was just for my pleasure and my enjoyment. It was me, taking control, making a decision regarding my life and what I wanted to do. I have never before done anything so completely self-centered. I doubt I ever will again. It was good.

I sleep the remainder of the plane ride home. I wake up when we touchdown.

TRACK NINE: WICHITA

At the airport, I call Robert to let him know I am back and he can come pick me up. He tells me he is on his way and then hangs up. He doesn't say "I miss you," "Glad you're back," not a damn thing. Words are not important I tell myself. I make my way to my last baggage claim. After getting my goods, I call Robert to make see how close he is to the airport.

He answers on the third ring, "Where are you? I had to circle the place twice. Now I'm coming back a third time."

"I'm sorry baby, I just got my luggage. I'm on my way out now. I should have waited to call you until I had everything. Then you wouldn't be wasting gas."

"Damn right. Then I wouldn't have gotten here too early," is his response. He hangs up in my ear before I can respond. There is no place like home.

As the SUV pulls up at the curb, he gets out and throws my well-traveled luggage in the back. "Did you have a good time?" he asks while he gives me a side hug that you should only use for semi friends. But what the hell. This along with an almost kiss in the vicinity of my nose shows that he really missed me I guess.

"Yeah it was great."

"Well I'm glad you're back, the kids have missed you. They're driving me crazy." The quiet ride home really suits my mood. As we turn onto the quiet street where we have lived for the past fifteen years, I feel the security coming back. We don't have to talk. We know each other so well. After twenty-seven years, what is there to talk about? I am happy. I am safe. This is the life I know and love. My world was on a tilt for two weeks. Now everything is right again. It is good to be home. I have not changed. Nothing has changed.

Robert parks the car in front of our quiet home. As we get out of the car, I notice Michael, the kid that lives a few doors away, riding his bike down the sidewalk. I believe Michael may have some issues that his mom encourages. He is about eleven and is very strange. I personally think he could grow up to be a mass murderer.

I also think he has some knowledge of why there aren't ever any stray animals in the neighborhood. Dogs don't bark at Michael and I have seen him at night digging in his back yard. I am not accusing him of anything; it could just be my naturally occurring paranoia, but hmm…, it does make me think. At least I am used to this crazy right here.

Today, he has on a full-fledged Superman suit, complete with boots and cape. His cape is flapping out behind him as if it were laundry hung out to dry in the wind. Each flap down brings the cape in dangerous proximity to the rear tire. Each flap up brings the cape higher than his shoulders. Does anyone but me see this as a recipe for disaster? I call to him "Baby, you need to watch out for your cape. It's getting mighty close to that back wheel."

His momma should have never let him come out of the house looking like a damned superhero reject. She could have butched up and said "Either Superman or the bike, but not both." But no, she lets him do whatever he wants. He will end up cutting off her toes and eating them like popcorn.

I always try to be kind to him so he will skip my house when he goes on his murdering rampage. In this vein, when he brings the cape up over his head and ties the ends under his chin, I just smile. He looks like the truly memorable. I continue on to my porch. His mother must really hate him or his father I think to myself. There really is no place like home.

Not surprisingly, all of my children are waiting at the house to welcome me home. There is chicken in the sink waiting for me to fry it. They were also kind enough to buy cabbage. They are not considerate enough to cut it so I can do the frying. In addition, hey, could I please do a skillet of corn bread? They start in on the fruit while I fix supper. Yes, I am needed here. This is where I belong.

"How was your trip?"

"Did you take any pictures?"

"It was great. I took pictures, but can't put my hand on the memory card for the camera."

When Rene, the oldest at twenty-five, pops grapes into her mouth I smile as an errant thought of New York skips by. I hope there is not a watermelon around or I am going to lose it.

Through the chain at my waist, I send Mr. M.O.P. a message, "I hope they don't see the you in my smile."

Lynn, the third child at twenty, is telling me about her job. She is shaking her hair that is straight, black and perfectly coiffed. She takes such good care of her hair, I think about another head of hair.

My message to him continues, "I have to make sure you don't come through in my smile."

May, self-absorbed at twenty-two and thoroughly spoiled speaks. Of course, all action must stop and all eyes should turn to her.

"Well I'm glad you're back I broke my gold chain and dad doesn't know where to go to get it fixed," she says in a petulant voice.

That comment brings back too many chain memories so I ignore her. I am back at home.

Afterwards as we eat they drone on about something, about them, about their lives. They finally leave. I am relieved.

Robert shortly announces, "Come on its time to go to bed." Because he declares it is bedtime, we go to bed. This is what I am used to. This is what works for me.

Our loving is a continuation of the last time we were together. There is nothing new or unusual. I am starting to count the strokes and figure I should add some excitement. I squeeze his ass and he immediately stops.

"What are you doing? You're going to make me lose my concentration," Robert tells me.

God forbid that should happen. Routine. Safe. I guess he missed me. He does not even notice the chain around my waist. As he rolls over, another stray memory appears.

Mr. M.O.P., this has to be my last thought to you. "I hope he can't feel the you on my body, can't feel the imprint of the places, your hands on my ass like a pair of panties, my body reaching out to you, for you."

The next morning, Robert is trying to wake me up. He calls me but only gets through to my semi conscious, to that place in my mind where Mr. M.O.P. and I are together on our spiritual level. It is a slice of time outside of time. Blending fantasy with reality until I can't define what happened from what I wanted to happen. We answer.

"Yessss," slowly like a question, with so much emotion, so much bass.

I open my eyes and notice my hands are on the chains at my waist, connecting us. I pray he doesn't hear the 'you' in my voice. No excuses, no recriminations. I am back at home where I chose to be. Two weeks. A lifetime. He must never ever hear the you in my voice.

Robert tells me "I'm going to work. It is time for you to get up. Daylight is burning. I'll see you when I get home."

Since Robert said so, it is time for me to get up. Time to rise and face my first day without "him." I unpack and store away the memories. I remove the chain from my waist to help me forget. I can feel it there like a chastity belt, only lighter, more enticing, and more wanted.

The cds of his music, the brochure from the Nautica Queen, a bottle of Jack Daniels, a shot glass from Tijuana, his golden heart, the memory card from the camera, the chains, the fabric Alita wrapped us in which still holds the scent of that sensual oil, the red corset and stockings.

I take it to the basement. It all goes into the big black trunk in the basement, at the bottom of the house. Far away from me. I don't know why I don't burn it all. But I put it in the basement.

I am back to myself now. Tomorrow, I go back to work again. I'll start my routine as though these past two weeks never happened. I know I will forget one day. It's for the best.

***

My Travel Tips for Wichita

Go somewhere else.

THE FINALE

Since those two weeks, I have not been able to listen to the fellows' music; it just makes me want to see him again. I might remember things that are best forgotten. I want to forget. Whenever the music comes on the radio, I make an excuse to change the channel.

I feel as if by listening to the music, I have a connection to Mr. M.O.P. I can't allow that to keep happening. If I listen to the music, I will see him, feel him. It is better, even if extremely painful, to make a clean break. It has been a little over a year, and the break though made, is far from clean. I still think of him sometimes when my mind drifts.

I am going to do something foolish tonight. He is playing about an hour away from here. I have to go and see. Just to make sure that I am truly over this I tell myself. If I would be completely honest, I would say that I am going to have the chance to be close to him again. It is too close to resist.

I don't use the ticket I know is there waiting for me to claim. I am late being seated. People probably think I am crazy wearing sunglasses at night with my floppy hat. I sit in the back, hoping he will not, can't see me. I feel pathetic, as though I am begging for scraps. Nevertheless, I need to see him just one more time. I always feel him when he is on my continent, over time and over space,

Again, he is fascinating to watch. I can tell he knows I am here. He left a message saying he hoped I would come. And he has been waiting. I see him looking in my direction and scoot lower in my seat. The connection is still there. I watch as he seems a little off, sensing my presence as I am devouring his. My hand goes to the chain that I put on around my waist.

His eyes find me and I can feel the sensation and tension. He gives me the head toss before leaving and going into his passion. It is as though we had never parted. This is a bad idea. I have to stand by my decision to end this because I don't want to feel the loss of another parting. I leave before the end of the gig so I will not be tempted to speak to him. I break away from the crowd and the him connection and make it to the door.

***

What If

It is two years later, a total of three years since my time with Mr. M.O.P. During the night, I sit straight up in bed. I would swear I felt him touching my face. I think I hear his voice telling me "Yessss" and kissing me on the lips. There is the unmistakable scent of Caesars Woman cologne in the air.

I go into the bathroom and cry for the past or for the future, I don't know. The missing him just caught me off guard probably. Then I dry my eyes and get back in bed with my husband, making sure to keep to my side of the bed. It takes me more than an hour to fall back to sleep.

On the way to work, I hear the news of his passing on the Tom Joyner radio show. Sybil, Tom, and Jay chat about him for a few minutes. They are reminiscing about his genius and their opportunities to see him in different places. He was also on the cruise once with them.

Then they move on to talk of other things. How can they talk about anything else when they have dealt me such a blow? I need some time for the world to stop and for me to catch up. He can't be dead. I still need to know he is here and a part of my universe.

I am unprepared for the emotions the announcement unleashes in me. He had a massive heart attack while being in his passion. He and the fellows were doing a set in Vancouver last night. He must have planned it. Vancouver was one of his favorite venues, he had once told me. He was dead before he hit the stage the onlookers said. How he must have loved that transition.

A few days later, by express delivery, I receive a large envelope with a lot of postage. Robert calls me at work to tell me I had gotten something in the mail. When I get home, I don't recognize the handwriting, or the city of origin. But wait a minute. It is from Paris. I only know one person there. Well, I don't actually know her, but we had shared a husband for two weeks. Curious, I open it.

Hello My Dear,

I want to inform you that he is physically beyond us both now. He made his transition. He wanted me to send this to you, so you would know.

You once asked me how I could live with him and accept that he saw others. The sharing of bodies is irrelevant if the other levels are not connected. Now the challenge is to live without him. He and I shared souls.

That is why I chose to share in his living and he in mine. We had magnificent decades together. I hope your time with him was equally fulfilling.

If ever you are in Paris, seek me. I will be here for you.

Now, let us celebrate his passing with joy.

Alita

With her handwritten note, she had included another folded paper. One that brings back a rush of memories. Thoughts of a time that was unmentionable. How could she have gotten this without him? Why didn't he burn it or throw it away?

IN YOUR PASSION

I saw you in your passion tonight
I watched you
Giving
Receiving
It was incredible to see
To hear
To experience
The music moved you in ways no human ever could

I saw you in your passion.
You were so there
 Away
Unreachable
I glimpsed your soul
It was so intense I wanted to cry.

We were as one
But I doubt you will remember my name.
Or my face in weeks to come
I am one of legions that have succumbed to your allure

But
I saw you in your passion tonight
And I thank you
For I will never forget

My writing to him of how I felt the first night I heard him play. At the bottom, he had written "Beloved, I never forgot. I'll see you next lifetime if not sooner." It was dated a month before his transition. It moves me so profoundly; I start crying and can't stop.

Robert comes in and sees me. "What's the matter?" he asks.

So I tell him. "This guy that played in a band died. I met him once and saw them play before."

"Who," he asks. I notice he is looking for a way to retreat.

"He was just a man who played in a band," I tell him.

"Oh, sorry to hear it," is his comment. He quickly moves out of the room and vicinity to escape my tears and the threat that I may need consolation or comfort from him. Security has its price.

I take the time to think about what I could say to Alita or if it was even appropriate to say anything. She had shared something profound with me, her husband. Maybe I can share a thought with her. I make a note of her address.

I think about what I had told Robert. It is not true that he was just a man in a band. He was so much more. The description is not fair to him or my time with him. He was so much more than a man who played in a band.

*****

Finding Passion

I go to look for what he was to me, in the basement where all of the memories reside. In the trunk, I remove the top two shelves of children's grade cards, pictures, plates of handprints. At the bottom of the trunk, I find him.

I am trying to get to the real memories, my memories for when I am by myself and missing me. The missing camera memory card, all of his music, it was in the trunk, just for posterity's sake. I never play them, even though I know they are there beating like a double drum. I can remember the sets, the places, and the connection. When I put them in the trunk upon my return, it was so very important that those connections be severed. Now?

I pull out the two discs that I had used to save my voice recordings and the notebook that comprised my diary from that time, that piece of my life that never saw acknowledgement or recognition. What I have avoided looking at since it was placed there in tears years ago. It is brought out amid more tears, again for what might have but not ever really could have been. I have to face him again. Two weeks, that was what we had, no more. Now never the hope, no matter how buried, no matter how secret the desire, for more.

He had called me several times. What if I had taken a telephone call? What if I had went again the next year or the year after, as he would request in his messages? In each message, he told me that there was a ticket at the venue with my name if I should change my mind. He would also leave all of his numbers, home and cell, here and in Paris just in case I wanted to call.

He told me he felt me the night I did give in to temptation and go. He saw me leave. If we had physically connected then, I would never have stopped. He would have given me three maybe four times in a year something I could treasure.

However, I believed I needed the safety of my own environment. Therefore, I made my decision. I don't really regret it when I am awake and the light is shining. However, in the middle of the night, when I get up to go to the bathroom and know in my spirit that he is on my continent, then, the fantasy invades.

The fantasy is always a replay of what a wonderful time I could have had with him three maybe four times a year. I try to rush back to bed, before I have the chance to regret. I know that I would never forget our two weeks any more than I could admit my deep affection for him. I sometimes Google him just to see his name, know where he was playing.

I also know I need to share him. Even from where he is, he overpowers me. Screaming for recognition, daring me to forget what we shared. More importantly, daring me to share what I found with him.

I pour a shot of Jack Daniels into my Mexican shot glass. I take out the chains for my waist and head. It is difficult, but I put them where they belong. On me. We are still connected on these levels. I add the genuine gold heart locket from Tijuana. I spray the air with the Cesar's Woman perfume, hot sex. I immerse myself in our memories.

"Yessss," I hear him say.

I find a pen and paper. What can I write about him, this man that I never even called by his name for fear that if I ever said it, it would come forth on its own accord. I remember that he never heard me say his name. Moreover, I remember how he said mine, with that wonderful accent. I remember feeling so alive and eager.

I can write about our time together. The time that I ran away and was never really missed. I can write about when I saw more of the country in two weeks than I had in damn near fifty years. No, I can't. I certainly can't write about a two-week interlude with a man who is not my husband. Besides, I don't want people to think I am a tramp.

I will write about his music. No, I can't. I don't know enough about music to write about his music. I will write a travel book. With him, I saw a bit of the world. We went from Cleveland to Tijuana. So, I put in one of his cds, grooving to him and the fellows in passion. I am transported, back to a club in Cleveland, watching, listening, and being. Touching the chains at my waist and my head brings the words dancing around in my head.

I release myself, open myself, and begin feeling, the prelude to writing. The words continue to come and I begin my journey anew:

***

Dear Diary,

I am so excited. I'm going on the trip of a lifetime. I will be traveling in Europe for two weeks. I have got all of my information together, all of my bed-and-breakfast stops, and my rail pass. I'm good to go. I've checked to make sure I have my passport. I don't want to be locked out of the country.

I think about all of the time we had spent together. All of the places and tourist activities we had experienced together. I continue to write, remembering, imagining. I rest from writing for a moment, letting the words swirl and slow.

Then to him, my muse, I send a prayer, along with a sincere appreciation for two unforgettable weeks. What may have been common to him was incredible for me. For that time, I tell him, "Thank you for sharing. Next lifetime? I sure hope so.

And on the whisper of the wind I hear "Yessss."

I lift my pen. Then once again, running away with him, I am truly finding passion.

ABOUT THE AUTHOR

Christy Cumberlander Walker is a proud mother of seven children she refers to as the magnificent seven. She was born, raised and continues to live in Ohio. Each winter she threatens to leave for a warmer climate.

This first novel is the culmination of a lifelong ambition sidetracked by children and careers until now. Follow Lynn in *Sensing Passion: Travels of a Fifty-five Year Old Divorcee*, available on Amazon.

She is currently working on her the final book of the Passion trilogy, *Embracing Passion: Adventures of a Woman,* where Lynn completes her travels.

An experienced mediator, arbitrator and facilitator, Christy enjoys providing dispute resolution services and delivering training worldwide.

Please let her know your thoughts about her book. You can write to her at:

Christy@christycumberlanderwalker.com

or visit her website:

www.christycumberlanderwalker.com